I0713364

The White Way
ISBN: 978-1-945307-02-7 (paperback)
ISBN: 978-1-945307-03-4 (ebook)

Book compilation and design by Rodney Schroeter

The Silver Creek Press
PO Box 334
Random Lake WI 53075-0334
rschroeter@silentreels.com

A Novel of New York's Broadway

by

Albert Payson Terhune

Illustrated by William Oberhardt

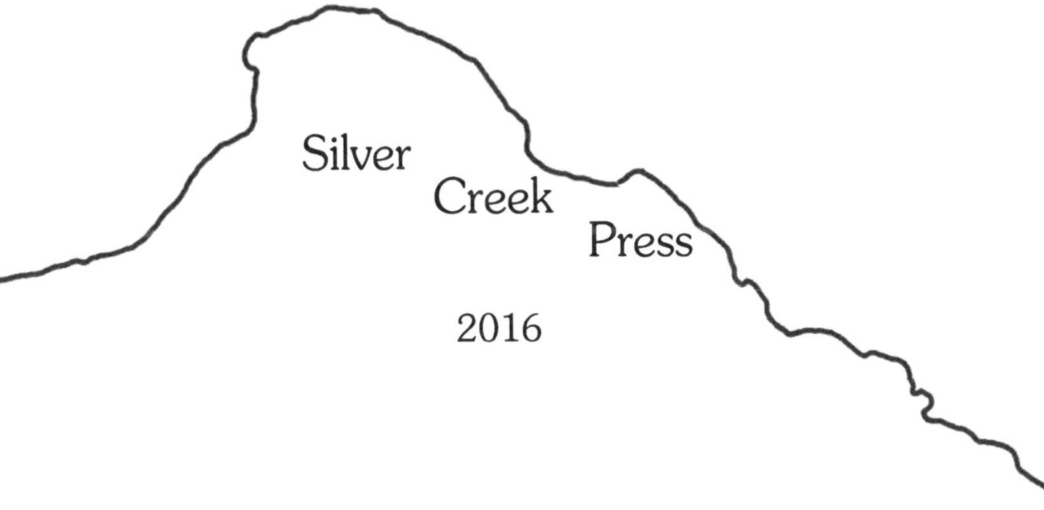

Chapter I

BEDLAM and the theaters turned loose their occupants at the same moment. The garish white line of Broadway, with its harrow-teeth of side-streets from Herald Square to the Winter Garden, was the glistering receptacle into which these two elements were dumped.

The air was ajar with carriage-calls, clanging gongs, the whiz of endless motors.

Nineteen New Yorkers out of twenty work with a delirious energy all day and, six nights a week, are in bed by eleven. The twentieth New Yorker and the stranger within the city's gates keep the lights agleam on that short central mile of Broadway and upon some of the twenty shorter parasite-streets that cling to its edges. So carriage-shouts and a metallic multi-roar that assailed high heaven—a swirl of sidewalk-crawlers and a jam of midstreet traffic, a pervasive reek of gasoline subtly blended with the effluvia of fifty different brands of sachet, a bewilderment of dazzlingly flaring light from signs and windows—these formed the raucous welcome accorded to twenty thousand theater-goers in general and to four theater-goers in particular at eleven o'clock one late September night last year.

The four theater-goers, whom we shall snatch at random from the twenty thousand, stood in the thronged lobby of the Hyperion, waiting until one of the side-street's fifty maneuvering automobiles should receive its call and move up to the bit of curb in front of the theater's awning. Stolidly the four stood, with all the long-learned patience of true New Yorkers, waiting their turn. And all four, through this same long experience, were blind to the fact that they were the collective target of more interested glances than were any of the hundreds of people who hemmed them in.

A newspaper reporter, who on his weekly "night off" had taken his New Jersey sweetheart to the Hyperion, piloted her a little way out of the sluggish human current that drifted streetward through the lobby, and brought her to a momentary standstill.

"Those are the people in the second row I was trying to make you see this evening," he told the girl. "They're at every first-night—especially Braith. And they're all Broadway celebrities. The long, dark chap with the nose is Dave Rodman, the big wine-agent. He's backing this show we've seen. The statue-built blonde with all the diamonds is Marion Kessel."

"The—*the* Marion Kessel?" asked his sweetheart in awe, her big eyes fairly devouring the gilt-haired woman in the flame-colored opera cloak. "The one who sings in comic operas and writes 'How to Be Beautiful' articles for the papers? I've seen her pictures, lots of times, but—"

"Yep, that's the one, the one and only. And she writes beauty articles too—at least, she signs them, and that's all we've a right to expect. The woman next to her, that one with the bronze hair and the slender figure, is Viva Russ."

"I never heard of her. Is she an actress too?"

"No. But she has more to do with plays' success than most actresses. She's an artist. And she's won a lot of fame by designing stage costumes and painting models of scenes and sketching stage-settings. She's rather a power, on Broadway."

"Why, she doesn't look a day over thirty."

"She isn't," said the reporter. "I don't believe she's that. But age and fame don't have much in common on this little street. It's the goods that count, and Viva Russ has got 'em. Take George M. Cohan, for instance. He was still under twenty-five when he—"

"Who's the fourth one?" interrupted the girl as the quartet began to move toward a newly announced car. "He has the strongest face I ever saw. He looks tremendously interesting and—what is the word?—magnetic! Who is he?"

"That?" queried her escort. "Oh, that's White-light Braith, of course. That's his circus-parade car they're piling into. He's the host, as usual. Braith—"

"Who?"

"Why, Magnus Braith—White-light Braith. You've surely heard of him?"

"No," she said a little crossly, "I haven't. I've heard of Diamond Jim Brady. Is White-light Braith the same as—"

"No—Diamond Jim is dead. But Braith is a good deal like him in a lot of ways. He's a chronic first-nighter, the way Brady was. And he works like a dog all day, as Brady did, and spends his

evenings and oodles of cash on Broadway. He buys four second-row seats for every first-night, and he has an eating capacity that would kill most men. He is as much a part of Broadway life as K. & E. or Churchill's. I've got an idea Braith started out by trying to model himself on Diamond Jim, but he's added a lot of new stunts as he went along, till now he's a character by himself. He—"

"Where are you going to take me to supper?" she asked, her thoughts straying foodward.

MEANTIME the violet-and-saffron limousine which the reporter had irreverently dubbed a circus-parade car was wriggling its way northward amid a chugging swarm of greater and lesser vehicles. It came to a skidding halt on the rain-whipped pavement, just beneath an electrically blazoned and many-hued glass peacock that jutted out into the thoroughfare some fifteen feet above the entrance to Rector's.

Magnus Braith and his three guests were received by the carriage-man, the coat-attendants, the head waiter and his myrmidons with the humbly affectionate welcome accorded only to Broadway notables and to visiting royalty.

As the party (the center of a tenderly solicitous little cloud of waiters) sought its table, fully as many interested eyes were turned upon it as in the lobby of the Hyperion.

All this was fame—the fame which Magnus Braith had so avidly craved, and which now he no longer noticed.

To-night, indeed, he was not in the mood to enjoy fame or anything else. The play whose première he had just attended was one in which he had been more or less financially interested. And it was a failure. Braith's trained acumen told him that. The merciless first-night audience had viewed it icily and then with coughs, yawns and feet-shufflings. It would not live out a fortnight.

Therefore Magnus Braith was blue and irritable—not that the loss of money would embarrass him to any great extent, but he sharply resented the slap administered to his much-vaunted theatrical judgment. He had picked a loser.

Glumly he looked up from the caviar which presaged the more solid part of the supper. Viva Russ was monopolizing the attention of Rodman, the wine-agent—whom, he knew, she cordially disliked. She was evidently putting herself out to be nice to him. Marion Kessel was talking animatedly to a pursy and beak-nosed little theatrical manager who had crossed to their table uninvited for a chat with the fair musical-comedy star, and who was bending, fatly, above her. The host was isolated. Then he devoted himself to the caviar.

Glancing up from under his bushy eyebrows, as he ate, he caught Viva Russ' gaze momentarily turned from the wine-agent and fixed on him. He

thought he saw in her level eyes a shadow as of disgust at his wordless enjoyment of his meal. Perhaps she thought a host should devote himself more to his guests and less to his food—even though his guests were ignoring him. And this new slur flicked him on the raw.

"She thinks I'm a boor!" he told himself surlily. "That's what she thinks. But what's *she?* It's just as bad manners for her to shine up to Dave Rodman, so's he'll get her a chance to do the designing for that new music-show he's backing. Yes," the train of morbid reflection bore him along, "and Kessel's just as bad—trying to make a hit with Arnheim for the lead in 'The Cabaret Kid.' She hates the sight of him. We're all of us truckling to each other or shoving each other for more room at the trough in this pig-pen we call Broadway."

HE speared his final oyster with a savageness that attracted even Marion Kessel's bovine attention.

"What seems to be the trouble, Magnus?" she asked, turning momentarily from Arnheim. "Diving for pearls among your oyster-beds?"

"No," he snapped crossly, watching the approach of the next course, "casting pearls before swine."

As he muttered the graceless words under his breath, she did not catch their import. And he had the decency to be glad she had not. He looked furtively across the table toward Viva Russ. And though her eyes rested on him with no expression whatever, he somehow feared she had heard, and he was ashamed. But when, presently, Viva spoke to him, for the first time since they entered the restaurant, her manner was so impersonally pleasant he was certain he had been mistaken.

"You ought to get Fernley to have a different color-scheme designed for that first-act set," she said. "I meant to speak to you about it after the act was over. It would make a world of difference if—"

"That's right. It would," he admitted. "But it's too late now. The show will be playing dead dog this time next week. And then it won't matter what the first-act settings were. They'll all be thrown into the storehouse."

"Poor things!" sympathized Viva. "Why, they'll be almost as badly off as your pearls."

"Pearls?" echoed Rodman. "Since when has Braith been buying pearls? And who's he been buying them for? I thought he was the only man in the crowd who hated jewelry."

"They weren't real pearls," explained Viva cryptically. "And"—with an innocent smile at the discomfited Braith—"perhaps the swine aren't really swine, after all. A looking-glass isn't the very best guide to life."

Rodman, understanding the meaning of not one word she said, mentally classified it, after his kind, as "highbrow stuff," and in panic steered the talk to less dreaded channels. Magnus Braith, however, slowly turned purple and retired smartingly into his meal. Nor did he volunteer another word until they rose to go.

AS the four passed out of the dining-room, Viva Russ dropped into step at Braith's side.

"I want you to do me a favor," she said.

"Most people do," he answered grumpily. "But you've sure taken a swell way to put me into a good humor beforehand."

"I don't try to put people into good humors before I ask them personal favors," she returned.

"No?" he queried in elephantine surprise. "Not even Dave Rodman? I s'pose you were so nice to him to-night just because you like his middle name and the fine way he treats his folks."

"No," she said with unembarrassed frankness, "I was nice to him because I want him to get me the chance to do the costumes for 'My Tipperary Maid.' You know that. He knows it. That's a professional favor, and it is just as legitimate for me to make myself pleasant to him as it is for a librettist to take him out to lunch or for you to tip a waiter. It's all in the day's business. Personal favors are different."

"And you've picked *me* for the personal one, hey? That's all right. I'll be glad to help you out. What is it?"

"In the first place I want you to drop Dave at his club and Marion at her house and then take me home."

"I was going to do that anyhow; it's the shortest route, and—"

"And then," she pursued, "I want you to come upstairs to my flat for a ten-minute talk."

"The favor seems to be the other way around," he answered less ungraciously. "I'm always tickled to have a chat with you. I'll be there."

"Thanks," she replied in the businessman tone he so hated in women; then she continued less brusquely: "I'm sorry I said that thing about pigs and looking-glasses. But honestly, you brought it on yourself."

"Oh, that's all right," he made awkward reply.

CHAPTER II

VIVA RUSS occupied exactly one ninety-eighth of the apartments in the Sydcroft Arms—a domiciliary beehive which teaches the art of compact living (or the canned life) on the corner of Broadway and one of the Seventieths. Leaving his chauffeur and his circus-parade car to stand in the rain, Magnus Braith escorted Viva indoors. Through an onyx hall and past a forest of almost-palms and around a very hideous and very huge yellow marble table, Magnus and his convoy made their way to a gilded elevator-cage. The cage's brunette aviator was clad in a uniform of gorgeousness not unlike that of a Prussian major-general.

Up ten flights the elevator whizzed them to a landing faced by eight numbered mahogany doors. Viva unlocked one of these and led the way into what the New Yorker who is lucky enough to afford such quarters wistfully calls home.

THERE was a soft, pinkish light glowing in the living-room; and even to Magnus' somewhat gaudy taste, the room itself was undeniably well furnished. That was Viva's trade. Magnus, despite his yearnings for brighter light and gayer colors, paid mental tribute to her triumph here as he plodded in at her heels.

Her aunt—a somewhat monkeylike little old lady with a pathetically perpetual smile—shared the home and was dutifully sitting up for her niece. But after a minute or two of excessively dreary conversation she left the room on some excuse and neglected to come back. This was her way.

"Well," announced Magnus, as soon as he and Viva were alone, "I'm here—like you asked me. How about it?"

"You can smoke, if you want to," said Viva. "I suppose I can't offer you a highball?"

"No, thanks," he refused. "I guess I'm about the only man on Broadway who doesn't even know the taste of booze and who hasn't any ambition to learn. But I'll eat a cigar, if you're sure you don't mind.

"Now, then,"—as he struck a match and proceeded to puff his cigar alight,—"I'm keeping you up. And you're doing the same thoughtful kindness for me. S'pose we get down to business."

"Do you know," observed Viva, frowning a little at his brusqueness, "you do dozens of kind things all the time, Mr. Braith? But you do them— as you're doing this—much as a man might beat a starving dog with a chunk of raw meat before giving it to him. It's none of my business, of course. But—why do you do it? If a thing is worth doing at all, isn't it worth doing gracefully? You make people feel ashamed to ask or accept anything from you."

"Most of 'em seem to go out of their way for a chance to be ashamed," he commented. "I notice, wherever I go, folks hang up the sign: 'Here comes the mark! Don't let him get away!' And neither do they let me get away. They strike me for favors and they act as if such a measly dub ought to be grateful to pay high for the bliss of associating with 'em. And—I keep on paying—and associating."

"Why?" she asked in very genuine curiosity. "I've often wanted to ask. Why?"

"Why not?" he scoffed, a tinge of sullen bitterness in his heavy voice. "What else is there for me? I don't like it. But I do it, because there's nothing else to do. They bleed me. But no set of folks, outside the Broadwayites, would bother themselves to come near enough to me to do even that."

"I don't quite understand."

"I guess you do. But, you're too diplomatic to say so. Here's the idea: I'm White-light Braith, ain't I? I'm thirty-seven years old. And no one's going to call you a liar if you say I could scrape together pretty near two million dollars in cold cash, at seventy-two hours' notice, if I was a mind to. But that's all I got. I used to think it'd be just about everything. I know now that it don't count much more'n a pair of deuces, in the real game. Till I was eighteen years old I never even had a collar on, and I never owned two suits of clothes or two pair of shoes at a time; I'd never been within touching distance of a glove. And I used to watch rich folks, and I used to swear I'd be one of 'em some day. And I am. If you want anything and want it enough, you get it. And a bum lot of good it does you!"

HIS rank cigar had gone out. He relighted it and went on: "Then, when I was puddling in the machine-shops, I invented that air-compression apparatus of mine. It's still making me richer every day. That's old history to you, I s'pose, if you ever were interested enough to ask anyone about my start—as it isn't likely you did. Well, I was so tickled over it all I wanted to make a splurge—like a man who gets his first pay envelope and wants to order a swell feed. I'd read in the papers about 'Diamond Jim' and some of the rest of the limelighters. And I figured that Broadway was the easiest place to get famous, when a chap had plenty of cash and nothing else. So I started in, and I got what I went for. I always have got what I want—except one thing. I only wish I could keep on wanting things after I get 'em."

"What's the one thing?" she asked, her curiosity piqued. "Do you mind telling me?"

"It's the one thing I've never been able to find on Broadway. And I guess it isn't to be found in New York. It certainly isn't by me. You'll only laugh if I—"

"No, I sha'n't. What is it?"

"A home—and all a home means to a poor gink that never had one. My suite of rooms at the St. Crœsus sets me back eight thousand dollars a year. And it's about as much like a home as a diamond flatiron is like a tenderloin steak smothered in onions. I want a home. And I can't find one."

"Everybody must make his own home," she said tritely enough, puzzled at the man's unwonted mood, "if he wants a real one. It can't be bought."

"That's just what I'm trying to tell you," he said wearily. "It can't be bought. That's why I can't get one. And I don't want anything else."

His alert, pale eyes darkened under their beetling thatch of brow. And his heavy voice took on a rumbling tone. He seemed half oblivious that he was speaking aloud, as he continued:

"A home means a wife. It's the wife who makes a home, if it's to be made at all. The man has nothing to do with it—except to kneel down and thank his God for it. I could marry any one of a dozen women, I s'pose. But I'd have to buy 'em. They'd be hard-faced and made up and as sophisticated as a barkeep. And they'd have a wife's true love for my bank-account. But they'd look on *me* like I was something the cat had brought in. Even if one of 'em was silly enough to care for me, she wouldn't be the woman I'd want to marry."

"What right have you to think," she challenged, "that business or a professional life makes a woman any less womanly or worthy or good than an untried woman would be? Ignorance and innocence don't mean the same thing."

"No?" he scoffed, roused from his reverie by her sharp interrogation. "Well, innocence and ignorance may both be lying around loose in the business world and in the Broadway game, but a fifteen-year search hasn't given me a look-in at either one."

"Thank you," she said, compressing her lips.

"Oh, no offense!" he assured her. *"You're* all right. You're straight and you're square, and you're a good enough friend. I kind of like you. But you're a business woman. That means, to me, that you're more like a man than a woman. You've stung me once or twice—and stung me fair—in theatrical deals. I don't hold any grudge. It only shows you were cleverer than I am. And my hat's off to anyone who is that. You're the best of the Broadway bunch. I'll grant you that.

"But it's a bunch I'm sick of. I want a home. I want to find a girl that's the kind of girl my mother used to be, out yonder in the country. Say!" he broke off, "I'm sorry I've been wasting your time with all this drivel. I've been keeping you up. And you couldn't turn me out, because the favor wasn't asked yet. I'm sorry. Go ahead and tell me the favor."

FOR an instant Viva Russ didn't speak. Her level eyes were bent inscrutably on his. Her face was a shade paler than usual. She was hotly indignant at this man's coarse appraisal of herself and her type. Yet the surprising glimpse he had given her of the blunderingly love-yearning boy that had always been wistfully lurking behind all Braith's middle-aged materialism touched her to the heart. And it silenced the angry retort on her lips.

"Not sore on me, for speaking so, are you?" he asked, uncomfortable at her wordless gaze.

"No," she said simply, "because you don't know any better. And I'm afraid—or rather I hope—you never will."

"Hope it, hey?" he growled. "Gee, you *must* be sore."

"No," she told him, "I hope it, because I'm not sore. I hope it, because I think it is better to go through life longing in vain for some beautiful thing than to attain it and then find it isn't beautiful at all. The Danes have a proverb: 'God save you from the Werewolf and from your heart's desire!' "

"But—" he protested.

"So now for the favor," she went on, pointedly unheeding. "My father has wished a budding playwright on me. Dad is a clergyman—I don't know if I ever told you—in a little place up in northern New Jersey. (He has eight hundred dollars a year and a parsonage and six children. That is why I went into business; *some one* had to pay the bills.) One of his parishioners wrote a play and brought it to him to read. Dad knows nothing at all about plays, of course. He hasn't seen one, since 'East Lynne.' But he read this, and it struck him as wonderful. So he sent it to me to read. I've read it. And Mr. Braith, it is the real thing. It is crude in spots; that is to be expected. But it simply bristles with cleverness. It has some tremendous situations. And there's a novelty, an originality, a charm about it, that fairly gripped me. You know, I'm not given to gushing. So when I say—"

"Nothing doing!" interrupted Magnus.

HE was once more the keenly impersonal man of business. The morbidness and the somewhat maudlin mood bred of it were both gone. This was the Magnus Braith whom his own financial world knew and respected.

"Nothing doing," he repeated. "I've heard the song before. And I don't care for the tune—not meaning to give you a short answer."

"Just as you choose," she said, striving to hide her disappointment. "But I am offering you the chance—the first chance—on a big thing. The play is going to score. It—"

"Miss Russ," he broke in, "the man or woman who says in advance that *any* unacted play is going to score is just about as wise and truthful as the guy who predicts what kind of weather we're going to have four years from next Saturday. No play is a success till it succeeds, and sometimes not then. And when it's written by a blithering amachoor—"

"I wrote to Dad what I thought of the play," she said, "and he showed my letter to the author. And she came to town the very next day—that is, this morning—with a letter of introduction to me from Dad. And she camped down on me here. I promised, for Dad's sake, to do all I could to get her play accepted, and—"

"And you thought it'd be easier to int'rest some fall guy in it, and get him to push it and maybe back it, than to turn it over to some play-broker to peddle?" he supplemented with heavy playfulness. "And you picked *me* out for the fall guy? Most people do; and most people are wrong. If it was a question of a personal loan, now, or a letter to a manager, or even a slice of interest in some promising show by a recognized author,—like that flivver we went to tonight,—I don't say but what I'd be glad to accommodate you. But it's twice as spectacular and ten times as easy to scatter my surplus cash from the top of Brooklyn Bridge as to sink it in a first play by some rube— or was it a rubette?—from the tall timber. In the one case I'd get good notoriety. In the other I'd get only the laugh. And I can get laughs cheaper than that. Good night, Miss Russ. Sorry to have took up so much of your time for nothing."

He got awkwardly to his feet. Viva did not try to stay him. In his progress toward the hallway he neared a pair of dark portières which separated the living-room from the bedroom adjoining.

The portières very slowly opened. A girl stepped into the living-room. On the threshold she caught sight of Braith and halted, embarrassed.

Magnus Braith, at sight of her, stopped dead in his tracks and stood eying the apparition in dull wonder.

Viva Russ glanced swiftly from Braith to the newcomer. And her eyebrows contracted as if in sharp displeasure or physical pain.

CHAPTER III

AGAINST the dark background the girl hesitated in the softly roseate glow of the light. Very young, she was—very lovely, very dainty. She had evidently just risen from bed, for her unbound fair hair fell about her in a shimmering cascade, from the crown of her little head to far below her waist. One tiny hand held across her chest the folds of the white negligee she had thrown on over her nightgown. Her bare feet were thrust into pomponed slippers. Her flower-face was flushed with sleep, and her big blue eyes were as starry as those of a newly wakened child.

"I'm—oh, forgive me, Miss Russ!" she faltered, her flush deepening. "I thought you were alone. And I wanted to ask—to—"

She made as though to draw back through the curtains as she spoke. Magnus felt as if a door to sunshine were about to be slammed in his face. He wanted to cry out: "Don't go! *Don't go!*" But Viva saved him the trouble.

"Come in!" she said, her voice unduly imperative and harsh. "Don't look as if you wanted the floor to open and let you through. Mr. Braith won't mind the way you look. In the theater world, a negligee is as conventional as an ulster. It's the *entr'acte*-interview costume of every actress. Come in."

Timidly, wincing a little at the older woman's roughness, the girl took a step forward; then she stood uncertain, looking in deprecatory appeal at the man, as if apologizing to him for appearing thus in his presence.

"This is Mr. Braith," went on Viva in the same curtly ultra-businesslike tone. "Mr. Braith is the gentleman I told you I'd ask about the play. He—"

"Good Lord!" sputtered Braith, finding his voice but no trace of his brains. "Are—are *you* the woman from north Jersey who came here to sell a play?"

"I'm Maida Standish. Yes sir," responded the girl bashfully.

The "sir" stung Braith into a realization that he was nearly thirty-eight years old—that this wonder-lass was twenty-one at the very outside, that she doubtless regarded him as a grandfather.

He pondered, vexedly, as to why this thought hurt him so. But now Maida was looking up at him with a new and childishly delighted interest.

"Oh!" she breathed, "I wish I'd known sooner that you were here. I was fast asleep. Then I woke up, and I thought I heard Miss Russ' voice. So I came in to ask if she—if she had been able to—You see, she said she expected to see you this evening, and she said she would ask you—"

"I did," cut in Viva tersely. "I did ask him. And he won't touch it."

The girl flinched, as if she had been sworn at. And noting her look, Magnus Braith felt like a child-murderer. In that moment Providence very definitely deprived him of sanity.

"Hold on! Hold on!" he protested. "Don't go running away with an idea like that, Miss Russ! I just said it wasn't always safe to launch a play by an unknown author. That was all, Miss Standish. And neither is it. But sometimes a play by a beginner scores big. In fact, if it wasn't for beginners, the playwright-game would 'a' died out long ago. Let's all sit down again and talk it over for a few minutes, if you ladies aren't too sleepy. Shall we?"

"Oh, thank you ever so much!" said Maida.

SHE looked around her in charming helplessness; then she discovered a deep leather chair close behind her and proceeded to curl herself up in it, one pink foot under her, the pompon toe of the other slipper peeping out from the billows of her negligee.

Her loosened hair shone like fire-gold in the lamplight, making an aureole around her little head. Magnus contrasted it with Viva's sleek, masculinely severe coiffure, and the girl's unconscious charm of manner with Viva's sudden acerbity.

"Jealous!" he told himself. "Jealous of a younger, prettier girl. Just like the has-been is always jealous of the comer."

"It's so good of you, Mr. Braith," Maida was saying, "to take so much interest in a bread-and-butter chit of a girl like me. And it's so good in Miss Russ and in her dear old father too. You see, I've always been so crazy to write plays. From the time I was ten years old, I've rummaged in Papa's library for them. He has hundreds of old ones. He used to collect them. And I read and reread all of them I could get my hands on. And—and something inside of me kept whispering: 'Write one! You can, if you try!' And at last I did. So, when Miss Russ and her father liked it, I just knew I'd have to come to New York and make play-writing my profession. But I was terribly frightened. And I had such a hard time persuading Papa to let me come. It wasn't till Miss Russ said I could stay here awhile with her, at her flat, that he'd consent. I didn't get here till this morning. Tell me, won't you—*has* my play a chance to succeed? Please tell me."

"I can tell you better when I've read it," replied Magnus, still in a daze. "But Miss Russ says it's fine, and Miss Russ is a pretty good judge. If you've got a copy of the 'script here, s'pose you let me take it home? I'll read it through before I go to bed, and I'll drop you a line in the morning and tell you my opinion. If it's any good at all, I'll do everything I can to get it across."

He tore his gaze from the girl's happily grateful face, to Viva, a little glad to have pleased Miss Russ by belatedly granting her favor.

But the gratitude in Maida's flower-face was not reflected in the older woman's. Viva's expression had seldom been so sphinxlike in its impassive sternness. Nor did she speak a word of thanks. But the verbal shower of appreciation wherewith Maida rewarded his offer was more than enough to atone to him for Viva's ungraciousness.

When, twenty minutes later, Magnus Braith descended to his waiting car and wet chauffeur, he carried in his breast pocket the bulky, blue-bound script of "Ropes of Sand, a Comedy in Three Acts, by Maida Standish."

CHAPTER IV

BRAITH read the 'script of "Ropes of Sand" before he went to bed. Then he began at the "Cast of Characters" and the amateurish pencil-sketch of the first-act set, and read the play clear through a second time.

His slowly returning common sense had told him, on the way home from the Russ apartment, that he had let himself in for many sorts of trouble. He had been dazzled into pledging himself to do all in his power for a novice's play. And fifty to one, the play would be impossible for production.

In this spirit of annoyance at his own folly he had gone to his study and begun the reading of the play. And before he reached the end of the first act, he was sitting rigid, eyes a-bulge, every faculty tense. He forgot the late hour, his surroundings, even the wistful little face that had burned itself into his brain. He forgot everything on earth except that he was reading a masterpiece.

For "Ropes of Sand" was startlingly original. It was carried up to its powerful climaxes with the skill of a Clyde Fitch. Its humor was delicious—dainty and elusive, yet obvious enough to evoke chuckles of mirth from a mind as cosmopolitan as Braith's. He was entranced. Here was a find; a marvelous find. Had his worst enemy been the author, Braith would still have been forced to admit the play's greatness.

"Little girl," he whispered, his alert eyes strangely soft, "you've got the

goods! You're the real thing. And I'm going to *make* you. And I'm going to try to keep the pig-pen from smirching you in the making. Then—then, if I can get you to care—to care just a little, little bit—"

HE got out of his chair and started toward his bedroom, taking off his coat as he went. Then he paused, stood still a moment, tossed his coat on a chair and yawned with fervid loudness—after which he slouched back to the table and rummaged idly in a drawer.

Presently, with a swiftness almost uncanny in so big a man, he spun about, facing an unlighted alcove room just off his study. His right arm was rigid. In it was the automatic pistol he had found in the drawer.

"Hands up, please!" he said cordially. "Way up! Now come in here and let's get a good look at you. Next time you hide in a dark room, don't stand where you're outlined against the window. Come on out, friend."

At his summons a shuffling of feet sounded from the alcove, and a man sidled into the study, arms gawkily upraised. The intruder was tallow-faced and thin, neatly dressed, perhaps twenty-five years old.

"Huh!" grunted Braith. "You're a swell breed of burglar, *you* are. Didn't even bother to dress for the part. In a get-up like that you couldn't get a job in a crook-drama at Woonsocket, R. I. I thought all you ginks wore caps and neckerchiefs. Where's your flashlight and your kit and your oxyacetylene?"

The thief grinned in fawning terror at the pleasantry and wriggled a step farther into the room. The light fell more clearly on his face.

"Why, hello, there!" exclaimed Magnus in jovial recognition. "If it ain't the night hallboy on this floor! Charlie Logan is the name, isn't it? What's the idea? Speak up, son."

"I—they canned me," mumbled the other. "The super fired me to-night for sneaking a smoke, on duty. I lost my pay in a crap-game. I—"

He hesitated. With the air of a teacher coaching a forgetful pupil, Braith prompted him:

"So you figured you'd pick up a little something to hock, so as to tide you along till you caught a new job? You knew where the master-keys of this floor are kept. And of course you picked *me* out, instead of any of the rest, for a visit. I've tipped you three times as much as anyone else has. So, pure gratitude made you drop in on me, instead of the others. I get you. But son, you're a bum burglar. Why'd you stick around? Why didn't you grab what you could and make a get-away before I came home? You must 'a' had oodles of time. I didn't get in till pretty near two."

The youth hesitated, fidgeting. Suddenly Braith grinned.

"I see," he said. "You read the Sunday papers, of course? They're your

Bible, like they are to all good New Yorkers? And you read in Sunday's *World* where it told about me always carrying a couple of thousand-dollar bills in the inside vest pocket of whatever suit I have on? So you were waiting for me to shed this vest and go by-by. Hey?"

His mouth adroop, Logan nodded.

"Now," approved Braith, "that showed sense. I'd picked you for a bonehead. I'm glad I was wrong. You've got a brain; even if it's the bum kind of brain that makes you risk Sing Sing for the sake of dodging park benches. What am I going to do with you?"

THE other had no ready answer. His loose lips twitched.

"Put down your hands if you like," suggested Braith, laying aside the revolver, "I wouldn't 'a' pulled a gun on you if I'd thought a second. I didn't see you, plain. Besides, my nerves were jumpy. I can break you in two with my bare fists, if I'm a mind to. Now what am I to do with you?"

"Mr. Braith," whimpered the lad, "if you'll just let me go, this time, I swear I'll—"

"On the stage and in the movies," rumbled Braith, ruminatively, "the gallant young hero reforms the bad, bad burglar. And the burglar gets to be his faithful servant and develops into a comedy character. In real life the guy turns the burglar over to the cops, and then he has to waste a lot of time in appearing against him in court, and all his friends make funny cracks about it. And the burglar's weepy mother, with a black shawl over her head, camps on his doorstep. Son, if everybody was put in prison who has tried to sting Magnus Braith, two jails would hold 'em all, and those two jails could be built easiest by running a high stone wall around the equator. Why should I send you to prison and leave the rest of 'em at large?"

"Mr. Braith!" gasped the thief, hope breaking his voice.

"Oh, chase out of here!" growled Braith. "Chase! And any time you want a list of folks to rob, call on me and I'll make it out for you. Here! Take this handful of chicken-feed along with you. It isn't the two thousand, but it's a week's living. And it's better than Sing Sing. Chase. I'm sleepy."

"Mr. Braith!" cried Logan, tears coursing down his pasty cheeks, "you're the—the—"

"Yes," cut in Magnus, "that's what they all say. Only most of 'em say it beforehand. G'night."

CHAPTER V

MAGNUS BRAITH was at his office desk promptly at nine o'clock next morning. Before he had slept, he had mapped out the course he intended to pursue with Maida Standish's play. Briefly, he had decided to back the play, and to rush it to an early production. He had been minded to call up the Russ apartment, on his way to the office and tell all this to Maida. But with memories of the rising-hours of most of his women acquaintances, he forbore to wake her from the deep slumbers of nine A. M.—even to tell her such good news. Instead, he condensed the tidings into a ninety-word telegram, which he dispatched on his way to work.

From nine until two, to-day, Magnus became a money-making machine, shutting from his overbusy mind everything not absolutely connected with his compressed-air apparatus business. By two o'clock the first rush of work was over. He lighted a cigar, stretched himself luxuriously, and sent his hungry stenographer out to lunch. And his mind, reacting from its five hours' steady strain, swung back with automatic immediateness to Maida Standish as he reached out and touched a push-button. For from two to three P. M., he daily kept what he called "open house." During that hour he would see anybody and everybody who might care to pay him a business-call.

To-day his first guest was a reporter from *The Telegraph,* to get his views on the preceding night's failure at the Hyperion. Magnus had foreseen this and had rehearsed the pungently drastic three sentences which he shot at the reporter—whom he then curtly nodded into outer darkness.

The second visitor was a picturesquely down-at-heels Broadway character who called with a heartrending tale of starvation, and who pointed to his rags in proof thereof.

"Nothing doing!" pronounced Magnus, halfway through the story. "Your boots are sound and their laces are new. Your collar isn't frayed. You haven't worn that tie three times. Collar and boots are where genuine hard luck hits a man first. Boot-laces and neckties next. Git!"

The fourth Magnus hailed with a grin.

"Well, Brother Charlie Logan!" he chuckled, "come around for another try at that two thousand, hey? Gee, but you've got perseverance."

Logan swallowed, twice; then he said:

"No sir. I came because you chased me away before I could thank you right. And I was making a baby of myself, besides, by blubbering. I came to-day, to tell you you're *white*—clear down to the ground, and—"

"And to ask for a temp'ry loan," finished Braith.

"No sir," contradicted Logan, "to tell you I got a job this morning—a job that pays me two dollars more a week than the other did. And I'm going to put by that extra two dollars every single week—so help me!—till I've paid back the fifty you gave me last night. Here's forty of it now. If you don't mind, I'll hold out the extra ten till I get my first week's pay. It's all I've got. Then—"

"Son!" broke in Magnus in genuine alarm, glaring at the money Logan laid on the desk, "if you do a thing like this, you'll rob me forever of my faith in human nature. Take that cash back! Forget it."

"I'm not going to forget it," said the lad stubbornly. "I was half crazy last night. I'd played the idiot. And the kid is sick, and all. And I had to have money, so bad, I went loony to get it. But—"

"Hold on!" Braith stopped him. "You said something about a kid. You're married?"

"I—I was married," said Logan uneasily. "We—we didn't hit it off just right. I had a little cash Father'd left me. She got an idea it was more'n it was. When that was gone, she went too. She left the kid. And I got the hall-boy job so as to keep him with me. I'd never learned a trade. He's a dandy too, that kid of mine. Pretty near two years old and as smart as—"

"Buy him some—oh, some caviar or gumdrops or something, with my regards," suggested Magnus, shoving the forty dollars toward his visitor.

Logan put his hands behind his back. "No, thanks," he declared; and turning, he almost ran out of the room.

"Hey! Come back here!" yelled Magnus.

But Logan was gone. Braith started toward the anteroom door in pursuit. Just then the telephone on his desk rang noisily. Shrugging his thick shoulders, as if dismissing a puzzle too deep for him, Magnus picked up the instrument.

"Hello!" he called.

"Is this Mr. Magnus Braith's office?" came the response.

And at the sound a mighty rush of joy swirled through Braith's chunky body, reddening his face, setting his quick eyes aglow.

"Why—why, Miss Standish!" he sputtered. "Why, hello!"

CHAPTER VI

AS Miss Standish spoke again and went on speaking, Braith's ruddy color receded; his face sagged like a sick man's; his eyes took on an aspect of something akin to horror. The man seemed stricken.

"No! no!" he called frantically, as the sweet voice at the far end of the wire paused a moment for breath, "no! You *mustn't!* You mustn't refuse. Why, it's all fixed. I wrote you that, in my telegram. Didn't you get it?"

"Yes, I got it. It just came. That is why I'm telephoning. I had to let you know right away. I was afraid you might come up here, or that you might go ahead with the arrangements, or—"

"That's just what I'm going to do," he told her. "I'm planning to stop on the way uptown and see a manager I know. I've phoned for an appointment. And then I'm coming up to Viva Russ' flat to talk things over and—"

"No!" she pleaded, a break in her words, "that was what I was afraid you'd do. So I telephoned. You mustn't."

"Mustn't?" he echoed, blankly. "But why in blue blazes not? The play's a jim-dandy—like I said in my telegram. And I'm going to boost it, from soup to nuts. I—"

"No!" she refused again, and this time Magnus became certain that she was crying. "I can't let you help me. I *can't.* Please don't make it so hard for me, Mr. Braith. And please, please don't think I'm ungrateful! Oh, I can't explain over the wire! And I don't *want* to explain at all. So please don't make me. Just let the whole thing drop. I—"

"Miss Standish," replied Braith, "if I'd been of the breed that lets the whole thing drop I'd still be pulling down eighteen a week in the puddling gang over to the Steel Works shops. This play means cash and fame for you. Last night you was kind enough to ask my help. Today—"

"To-day," she cut in, her voice choked with the effort to fight back sobs, "today, I can't take your help. Won't you please understand how grateful I am—how unhappy I am—"

"No," he rasped, "I won't. And I can't. If you won't explain over the phone, I'm coming up there to make you talk it out with me."

"No!" she refused in terror. "You mustn't. There's nothing that can be straightened out. Besides, you couldn't come here, now. Viva isn't at home. And her aunt has gone out for the afternoon too. I'm all alone. So you couldn't—"

"It's what I'm going to do," he declared. "I—"

"But I can't see you!"

"That's up to you. But if you're the fair-and-square girl your eyes say you are, I believe you'll be white enough to tell me to my face why you're throwing me down. I'm coming up, anyhow. I'll be there in half an hour. I can't force you to see me, but I believe you're square enough and kind enough to do it."

HE hung up the receiver. He felt sick and dazed and wholly bewildered. All this was beyond his ken. People angled and maneuvered for the use of his money and influence. Yet this country girl was refusing both. It didn't make sense.

He set down the telephone-instrument and started for the outer door at the pace of a man running to a fire. And halfway to the door he collided with the next of his "open-house hour" guests.

The latest arrival was an obese and bald and bilious man about town whom Magnus, at best, disliked, and who had long since formed a habit of running to Braith with all his myriad woes.

"Magnus!" wailed the bold one right dramatically as Braith caromed off, breathlessly blasphemous, from the collision, "Magnus, old chap, she's left me! I spent twenty-seven thousand dollars on that woman in less than two years! I can prove it by my books. Twenty-seven thousand, and some cents! And now she's left me! Gone back to—"

"Oh, go buy another!" snarled Braith, deftly eluding the pudgy outstretched hands that sought his coat-lapel.

He brushed past the gaping visitor and dashed through the anteroom, pausing only to grab his hat from a nail.

"Mr. Braith!" a clerk called after him, "Mr. Gurney just rang up. He'll be here at three sharp to see you about those C. G. & X. loans. He's decided to take them over. And—"

"Tell him I'm dead," shouted Magnus, as he sprinted for the elevator.

With no concern at all that in the space of thirty seconds he had made an enemy of one man and had thrown away a brilliant business opportunity offered by another, Braith boarded the nearest subway express. Well inside the stipulated half-hour he was at the numbered door of Viva Russ' flat. He had not troubled to send up his name—nor, as the hallboy recognized him, had it been required.

"Miss Standish?" queried Braith, of the maid who answered his ring.

AS he nervously tramped the length of the little living-room, a minute later, Maida came in.

She stood on the threshold shyly, as she had done, last night. But this time there were faint traces of weeping around the starry blue eyes, and her manner held sorrow and constraint rather than mere embarrassment.

Magnus sprang forward, hand outstretched. For a barely perceptible instant she seemed to hesitate before giving him her white little fingers. And she withdrew them almost at once. There was a look akin to fear in the gaze that tried so bravely to meet his.

"Now, then," demanded Braith abruptly, "what's up? Thanks for seeing me. But I knew you would. What's wrong? Tell me."

"I'd—I'd so much rather not," she evaded, miserable and trembling. "It can't help. Why did you come up here, Mr. Braith?"

"To straighten things out," he made sturdy reply.

He was looking closely into her troubled face. In her trim tailor suit and with her fair hair piled high on her well-poised little head, she looked scarce eighteen.

"I'm so sorry you insisted on coming here!" she was saying. "It can't do any good. It only makes me unhappy. And—and it forces me to make *you* unhappy, too. And I hate that, worst of all, for you've tried to be so kind to me."

"Let's have it," he demanded briefly. "The reason, I mean. You owe that to me. We can attend to the rest later. Fire away."

She had seated herself on the extreme edge of the divan. She was nervously twisting her fingers together, and her long-fringed lashes were lowered. For a moment she did not speak. Then, glancing up at him, she began:

"I told you how much this meant to me, Mr. Braith—this play of mine. For a whole year I worked over it and lived with it and dreamed of it. And as it began to shape itself at last, I felt as Michelangelo must have felt when he saw the ugly block of marble begin to turn into an angel under his chisel-blows. Then when the play was written, it seemed to me I could never get it produced. You see, I had read all about the difficulties a novice has in—in—"

"In breaking into the game," supplemented Magnus. "But that isn't—"

"And I had no money or influence or friends to push it for me. So, last night, when you said you'd try to help me, I—I—oh, I didn't know anyone could be as happy as I was all night. Then, this morning—"

"Well?" he asked anxiously, as she hesitated.

"Then this morning," she went on with manifest difficulty, "I found, all at once, that I couldn't take any help from you, Mr. Braith. Then came your telegram—and then—and then—"

"Why couldn't you take any help from me?" he insisted. "*Why* couldn't you?"

AGAIN she hesitated, but seeming to nerve herself as for an ordeal, she went on, speaking rapidly and looking at the floor:

"When Viva told me she was going to speak to Mr. Braith about my play, I didn't pay much attention to the name. I supposed you were just an influential friend of hers, or perhaps a manager. I thought so, till this morning. Then—"

"Well?" he queried in dire perplexity.

"Then, this morning," resumed Maida, "after Viva had gone downtown for the day, I got to talking to Mrs. Miller—her aunt, you know. (She used to live next door to us, at home.) And she happened to mention you as Magnus Braith. I'd never dreamed that you were Magnus Braith—*the* Magnus Braith."

She stopped again, flushing. Her bronze-pointed toe was tracing the pattern of the Persian rug in front of the divan.

"What difference does *that* make?" challenged Braith.

"Mr. Braith," she replied with apparent irrelevance, "I've said my prayers every night of my life. And this past year, every night, I've asked God's help with this play of mine—asking Him to grant it success and to make it a power for good in the world. I have prayed so hard for it!"

She looked timidly at him as she paused. It was as though she dreaded ridicule. A light, almost of reverence, was in his eyes. And he said shamefacedly:

"I've done that same thing, every deal I've gone into, since I can remember. And I'd as soon—as soon think of going to bed without my pajamas as without saying my prayers. I don't go blatting about it to the folks I know, for they wouldn't understand. And besides, it's none of their business. But I'm saying it to *you,* so's you'll know I feel like you do, about such things. But what's all that got to do with—"

"How can I expect a blessing on my play," she went on, nerving herself again to the effort, "if it owes its success to a man like yourself?"

"What's the matter with *me?"* he asked, surprised.

"That is between you and your own conscience, Mr. Braith," she said gently. "Forgive me, if I hurt you—but I have heard about you and read about you, even at home. And my father once said you were perhaps the wickedest man in all New York. He—"

"What does your dad know about me?" cried Magnus in a gush of indignation. "And for that matter what do the folks know who write the newspaper rot he takes his notions from? They call me White-light Braith. And when they're hard up for space in their Sunday editions, they vamp some merry wheeze about my gambling away a million dollars at a sitting, or drinking six quarts of wine at one dinner, or shooting at some Broadway rival, or beating up a chorus-girl, or paying one hundred thousand dollars for a necklace for some one else's stage-wife, or backing a red-light resort, or eating four meals in one, or—"

"That is not my affair, Mr. Braith, but your own. All I know is that I cannot accept help from such a man. I cannot use, for my play, money that has been earned as yours has been earned. I—"

"What's the matter with the way mine is earned?" he demanded. "My Compressed Air works are run on the square. And—"

"I was not speaking of the money you earn in business," she corrected, "but of your other means of wealth."

"I haven't any others," he declared. "All the rest is outgo. If you're thinking of those slimy stories about my backing gambling-houses and red-light places and all that—why, they're a lie, from first to last. I didn't sue for libel on 'em because they didn't do me any hurt and because I don't care a hoot what my fellow-man thinks about me. But I do care a whole lot what *you* think, Miss Standish. That's why I tell you they're all a bunch of lies, those stories about me. Yes, and about my drinking and gambling and beating up people and all the rest. The stories about my eating are mostly true. I eat, because I like to eat—and because, when I was a kid, I used to have to go without it, oftener'n not. But my money's as clean as any other man's—yes, and my life as clean as your own father's, too—if he's a normal man and not a stained-glass saint. Believe that or not, just as you like. It's God's truth."

The very roughness of his fierce-spoken reply seemed to touch the girl. She looked up at him again, her big, wondering eyes searching his very soul. Magnus Braith continued:

"One man finds his fun, after work-hours, in collecting musty books or chipped porcelain. Another man finds it in stamp-albums or in raising blooded stock and such-like. I find mine on Broadway. At least, I used to. I've been dog-tired of it, for years, now. You see, Miss Standish, it's like that with me. At first the starved ex-newsboy used to love all that notoriety. Then the business man thought it helped advertise him. For a long time the *real* me has been sick of it, but I never knew till to-day what a lot of damage it was doing me with the only sort of folks I care about standing well with.

"Miss Standish!" he broke off, forcing her gaze to meet him, "I've turned my soul inside out for your benefit, this past half-hour. You've seen farther into it—whether you cared to or not—than anyone else ever has. And maybe you've seen more, too, than I was ready, quite yet, to let you see. Now tell me straight: do you believe me or don't you? Do you believe I'm the flashy crook and all-around rotter you was led to think I was, or do you believe I'm a fairly clean, well-meaning dub, whose cash is no more tainted than your pastor's? I ask you straight."

FOR an instant she did not answer; her gaze still held by the compelling frenzy of appeal in his. Then all at once the cloud of trouble lifted, as by miracle, from the blue of her eyes, leaving them aglow with a new and wondrously soft light. The illumination of her whole face struck him spellbound, silent.

"Yes," she said very gently, her hand finding its way to his, "yes, I do believe you, Mr. Braith. I don't know just why I do, for you've always been one of my detestations. But I do. I never thought I should learn to trust in you like this."

"I can prove—" he sputtered, delighted beyond expression.

"There is no need," she told him. "A woman either believes, or else she doesn't. No one knows why. Not even herself. She gives everything or nothing, for no better reason than because some blind instinct tells her to. She obeys that instinct because she knows it can never be wrong. That is why I believe in you—and why I—I beg your pardon."

"My pardon? For what?"

"For behaving as I did," she said contritely. "For believing things against you, without hearing your side of it."

"Let's forget about it, sha'n't we?" he soothed, his own voice none too steady; his heart pounding with bliss, at her childlike avowal. "You could 'a' spoken to me and thought about me a whole lot worse than you did; and it would 'a' made up for it all, just to hear you say you believe in me and—and like me. Gee, but I was pretty miserable for a while. You see, Miss Standish!" he added, "I've never stopped believing women were the greatest masterpieces the Lord ever turned out. And yet I've never met one of 'em that was what I believed God meant a woman to be—never till I met you. You see, I've had no chance to know any of 'em but the business kind and the purchasable kind. And neither type is what I want. I—I don't s'pose you're old-fashioned enough," he ventured bashfully, "to think a home is better than a career."

She laughed. It was a very pretty laugh.

"Why, Mr. Braith," she said, "to a genuine woman, I think, a home *is* a career. It is going to be mine, I know."

"Tell me," he begged, "what—what is your idea of a home?"

"A little house in the country," she began, her voice dreamy, her eyes half shut. "And plenty of housework and cooking and sewing to do, and—some one I'll love, to do it all for."

"This—this some one you'll—love," stammered Braith, "he—I s'pose he ain't picked out yet?"

"I'm not quite twenty-one," she laughed, "and I've known so few men.

Why, in all my life I've never talked to any man as I've talked to you to-day. I don't know why. You'll probably think I'm ever so foolish."

"I think you're ever so wonderful!" he blurted. "I never met a woman who wasn't more interested in cars and clothes and jewelry than in rustling a good supper for Hubby."

"Cars and clothes and jewelry," she repeated, musingly, "they'd be nice, too, I suppose."

"That play of yours," said Braith, "is due to get them for you, anyway. Want to hear the arrangements I'm planning for it?" he added, forcing himself back to earth with an effort.

"Yes! Please!" she cried, all eager interest at once.

For half an hour they talked, he sketching concisely his campaign, she listening closely, and sometimes asking a question or making a suggestion which, if showing inexperience, showed also a sound common sense and a quick brain. Braith was overjoyed.

When he rose to go, he said:

"I tell you, that little play is going to hit the old street like a rose-garden breath hits a slum. It'll make 'em sit up. Your fortune's as good as made before the first curtain."

"But if it *should* be a failure," she suggested. "Just think of the loss to you! All the money you will have risked and lost! And it will be my fault for—"

"Don't you go losing any sleep over that!" he assured her. "That play's going across, and it's going across *big!* And even if it didn't—well, I won't be the loser, in the end, on any partnership I make with you."

He held her hand very much longer and very much more tightly than was really needful, when he said good-by. And he went out into the noise of the street, muttering to himself:

"She—she makes me feel, sometimes, like I was in church! She has the eyes of a saint, that girl has. And—Lord, but what a picture of a home! A home—her and me!"

Left alone in the flat's pretty living-room, Maida Standish looked in elfin happiness after the departing guest. Presently her flower-face broke again into a wondrous tender smile. And her lips parted in half-articulate speech.

"One of them is born every minute," she quoted to her likeness in the mirror, "—but they must have used a whole month's supply on him."

Then she rummaged in her trunk for a cigarette. She felt that her labors of the past hour entitled her to this usually forbidden comfort.

CHAPTER VII

AS he reached the summit of the subway steps, Magnus Braith was hailed by a woman who was just emerging from that domain of minimum atmosphere and maximum speed.

He turned, to see Viva Russ. He was sorry to meet Viva—to meet anyone, indeed, who would rouse him from the roseate reverie wherein he had wrapped himself. He jerked his hat clumsily from his head, slapped it instantly into place again and with a brief word of greeting, started down the steps. But Viva, evidently, was not minded to be shaken off like this.

"What brings you Farthest North at four o'clock in the afternoon?" she demanded in genuinely cordial welcome. "I thought you never left your desk till five."

"I've been up to your place," he responded with gruff sheepishness.

"What a pity I wasn't at home! I'm sorry. Let's turn back now, though. It's lucky I happened to catch you. Is there any news about the play? Have you had a chance to read it yet?"

As she volleyed the staccato sentences, she set forth briskly along the walk in the direction of her apartment-house. Thus he had no choice but to fall grudgingly into step and to accompany her.

"I didn't come up there, to see you," he said, ungraciously. "I came to see Miss Standish. I wanted to talk over some plans about the play with her. Of course, it's good to see you too. I—"

Viva flashed a sudden look up at him; then she asked as suddenly:

"Did she send for you?"

On the instant, Maida's appealing eyes and her plea that he pledge himself to silence as to her summons sprang into Magnus' thoughts. And glumly resenting the query, he was at once on guard.

"Send for me?" he replied in really excellent surprise. "Why in blazes should she 'a' sent for me? She don't seem just like the kind of girl to send for folks to call on her, does she? I went there and had a talk about the play, so I could get her consent to a lot of details I'm to talk over with Benson when I see him at five-fifteen. I read the play last night, like I said I would. And it's a corker—sure-fire. I'm going to back it to the limit."

"Yes?" said Viva with a curious dearth of enthusiasm. "Maida will be glad, I know. And I think you will make a good thing of it for both of you. Are you going to try to get it on, this season?"

"Before New Year's," he replied, noticing and wondering at the odd change in her manner from the cordiality of a few moments earlier.

"That will mean quick work," she commented.

"It'll get *quick* work," he said. "That play is worth sudden action. No use trailing it along for a year before we do anything."

"Can you get a theater?"

"Benson will see to that—his own theater, the Halcyon, most likely. I'm turning over the work to him, on commission. In a town that has five failures to one real success, there's never any trouble about the right people getting some good theater pretty much any time they want it. You know that. Good actors, too—though this 'Ropes of Sand' play looks to be as near actor-proof as anything I ever read."

They had reached the ornate entrance of the apartment-house, and halted.

"Won't you come in?" asked Viva, a shade of wistful appeal in the question.

TEMPTATION seized Braith as he conjured up a vision of Maida's pretty joy at sight of him. But he wisely refused, realizing that two visits in one afternoon might strain the welcome of so new a suitor as himself.

"I guess not," he answered. "Thanks, just the same."

"Mr. Braith," said Viva impulsively, laying her neat-gloved hand on his arm as she spoke, "I like you. I like you very much indeed. Up to last evening I've never really felt I knew you. But I saw a side of you last night that I'd never even suspected was there..... I'd—I'd like to help you, if I might."

Surprised and touched at such a demonstration from the wontedly reserved woman, he tried to stammer some kind of thanks. But she cut him short:

"If I were like other women, I could be of use to you by putting you on your guard against—against all sorts of things. But I'm afraid I'm more like a man in not being able to be catty, and in not saying things I can't actually prove—about people. But I wish I could help, and I'm sorry I can't—because—because I like you and because you're too much of a man to be allowed to suffer needlessly. And that's just what I'm so afraid you're going to do. Good-by."

After this most inexplicable and most uncharacteristic speech, Viva turned, before Braith could answer, and hurried indoors. If he had not known better, he would have fancied there was a hint of tears in her level gray eyes.

CHAPTER VIII

NEXT morning a half-bushel or so of orchids were delivered to Miss Maida Standish with Magnus Braith's card. Late that afternoon a fearsomely ornamental ten-pound box of candy arrived. Magnus Braith was laying siege in due form. And daily the lavish shower of gifts continued. Daily, too, Magnus found pretext to call at the apartment, to discuss details of the play.

Presently rehearsals began; and these diurnal horrors gave Magnus still further opportunity to see Maida. He included Viva and herself, now, in nearly all his famous little theater-and-supper parties. He made occasion to call her up, on the telephone, at least once during every twenty-four hours.

And for Maida's sake he was making pitiful efforts to curb and soften the roughness that was a part of himself. His costumes and his big voice were far more subdued than of old. He sought out his occasional defects in English and tried to amputate them. Secretly he struggled to read—and fell asleep over—the books of verse and of philosophy he had heard Maida praise.

The only note of discord was supplied by Viva Russ. From the beginning, her behavior toward Maida was of cold civility. Her attitude toward the play was one of impersonal interest. Magnus she treated at times with what seemed an almost pitying kindliness. At other times, she was scarcely civil when she chanced to be present during his calls on Maida. Braith noticed, wondered and at last drew his own conclusions. Manlike, having drawn these conclusions, he wasted no time before taxing Viva with them.

His chance came late one afternoon, when Maida had not yet come back from rehearsal. Viva had just returned from work and was glancing over her new-arrived mail, when Magnus Braith's name was brought in. Magnus himself followed his card immediately into the living-room.

"I wanted to talk to you about Maida—and me," he said almost at once.

"Yes?" she said evenly, after an imperceptible pause.

"Yes," he replied, his thick eyebrows beetling. "It isn't a thing I care to talk about, but I've got to. I notice you don't seem to like me to come here, so much, to see Maida. And it set me to wondering—till I got the answer."

She had made as though to speak; but she changed her mind. And he went on:

"I know the sweet-scented reputation I've got on Broadway. And I know how Broadway gossips hop at a conclusion when they see a man like me rushing a girl like Maida. And I take it, you think I'm planning to live up to my reputation. Well, I'm not. I just wanted to let you know that, straight. I'm playing square, and I—"

"You don't need to tell me that," said Viva, her clear voice slightly muffled as she leaned down with elaborate care to pick a thread from her skirt. "I know you're playing square. I know you couldn't play any other way if you tried."

"It's white of you to say that," he commented gratefully. "I'm sorry I got you wrong. I figured it was part of the rotten way New Yorkers size up such things. But if you know I mean all right, by her, why in blazes do you act sore at my coming to see her?"

"I am not," she denied. "I didn't mean to seem inhospitable. How is the play coming on?"

"Fine!" he exulted, switched from the track by the more compelling theme. "Fine and dandy! It acts even better'n it reads. You ought to blow in to one of the rehearsals. Benson's earning his money, too. I'll say that for him. We're opening on Christmas night. I s'pose Maida told you?"

"I saw Dave Rodman yesterday," she said. "He told me he heard, through Benson, that you are spending a fortune in order to give it a wonderful production."

"I am," Braith assented. "And it's worth it. Fifty thousand dollars—easily that much—before the curtain goes up. And another fifty thousand, if it's necessary, to keep it going till it catches on. Because it's *bound* to catch on."

"A hundred thousand dollars in all?" she gasped. "You are preparing to risk that enormous amount on one play? Why, even if it is a tremendous success—"

"It's going to be!"

"Even if it's a tremendous success, can you make any profit on such an outlay?"

"Yes," he answered in strange fervor. "The grandest profit any man ever made."

"I don't understand."

"But you're going to," he said. "Because I'm going to tell you. I don't know why I blab about it to you; for I haven't told it to a soul. I'm pretty deep in love with Maida—like you've of course guessed. But maybe you haven't guessed she is just about the proudest little thoroughbred on earth. Well, she is. And she's poor. I kind of sounded her out, one day, without her suspicioning what I was driving at. And I got a pretty straight line on her ideas. If this play of hers should fail, she'd feel she was too proud to marry a chap with a lot of cash. She'd think it was too much like grafting. She said as much. If it succeeds, she'll consider herself rich enough to marry anyone she chooses to marry. That's why it's going to succeed. When it succeeds, and not till then, I'm going to ask her will she marry me. I guess she understands *that*, too. I'm putting this play on, with a lot more expense than it really needs, because all that helps. And I'm going to spend an extra five thousand dollars a week, if I've got to, to bring audiences there for ten weeks. There's a way of fixing such things. And Joe Leblang will help. By the end of ten weeks Maida'll be dead-sure it's a hit. And then—"

He checked himself, as if ashamed of his boyish outpouring.

She was listening to him with an odd mingling of cynicism and of half-motherly pity. He saw that her gray eyes were misted and luminous.

"What's the matter?" he demanded brusquely.

"The matter?" she repeated in startled evasion. "Why—why, nothing at all. I hope it will all turn out as you want it to. At least, in the way that will make you happiest."

"You don't think I'd be happy if she'd say yes?" he cross-questioned. "Why, I'd be just the happiest man on the whole footstool."

She said nothing.

"You don't think so!" he challenged. "You think I wouldn't be."

"With all my heart," evaded the poor girl, "I hope you would be."

He was quick to catch the evasion. And his wrath blazed hot.

"I know what's the matter with *you!*" he stormed. "You're jealous!"

"Jealous?" she echoed, yet more in startled timidity than resentment.

"Yes, jealous!" he accused harshly. "You're jealous because she's younger and prettier and sweeter and womanlier than you, and because Broadway hasn't smeared the first bloom off of her, and because she's due to score a hell-roaring success, while you've got to plod along for a bare living. You're jealous of all that. I've seen it, from the start. It's the jealousy of the professional for the amachoor, of the older woman for the younger girl, of the wise for the innocent. That's what it is! You Broadway women and business women have had your illusions and your youth battered out of you, and you can't appreciate a girl who hasn't. So you sulk at Maida's good luck. Well, go ahead and sulk, if you like."

HE pulled up abruptly. He had said more than he had intended to say. For the first time in his life, he had spoken to a woman with downright brutality. And he was ashamed. He prepared himself for a sharp tirade from Viva—perhaps for a furious command to leave her house.

But the storm did not rise. To Braith's amazement the mist in Viva's sorrowful eyes had turned to tears which rolled unchecked down her suddenly pallid face. Her whole attitude was that of one who shrinks from a beating. He felt like a brute. He could scarcely bring himself to meet the piteous look in her swimming eyes.

"Oh, say!" he exclaimed in clumsy contrition. "Don't take it like that, Viva! *Don't!* I didn't mean to hurt your feelings. You're—you're all right, Viva. I'm sorry!"

He found himself patting her shoulder in rough consolation. Viva turned abruptly away, walked fast to the window and stood for a minute looking out, her back to him. Magnus, remorseful, followed her.

"Please don't cry," he entreated. "I'd a lot rather have you be mad at me."

"I'd—I'd *rather,* too," she said with a queer little catch in her breath and with her head still consistently averted. "And I don't know why I'm not."

Then Maida came in, aglow and vibrant. And there were more interesting things to talk about than Viva's unwontedly softened frame of mind.

CHAPTER IX

CHRISTMAS night—the night of the première of Maida Standish's play, "Ropes of Sand," at the Halcyon Theater.

Christmas had been a day of mixed feelings to Magnus Braith. At eight o'clock in the morning a glittering little jewel of an electric runabout had drawn up in front of the apartment house where Maida lived. A chauffeur had ascended to the Russ flat and there had delivered to Maida a note and a tissue-covered box.

The note set forth the fact that the electric runabout was a Christmas present to her, with a billion good wishes from Magnus Braith, and that the chauffeur was detailed to teach her the simple art of running it. The accompanying box contained a dainty necklace of pearls and aquamarines.

At nine o'clock in the morning, Magnus received a sweetly and embarrassedly regretful note from Maida, to the effect that his two gifts were marvelous and that she did not know which of them she loved best— but that she felt it would be wrong for her, under the circumstances, to accept either of them. So she was returning them herewith, and she just hated to do it, and so forth.

Magnus talked to her in eloquently frantic appeal over the telephone for nearly an hour; at the end of that time he had the pride and delight of breaking down her fragile barriers of conventionality and of inducing her to accept his presents.

At ten o'clock in the morning he was amazed to receive a visit, at his rooms, from Charlie Logan. More than a month earlier Logan had mailed him the last two-dollar installment on the ten-dollar debt, with a brief note of renewed thanks and with the information that the ex-hallboy was doing well in his new job.

To-day Logan stood just inside the hall door of Magnus' suite at the St. Crœsus. The visitor was clearly under some strong emotion and found it hard to speak.

"Merry Christmas!" Braith hailed him. "How's the kid? Santa Claus get around to his stocking this year?"

"Yes!" Logan explosively broke his embarrassed silence. "Yes, Mr. Braith! Santa Claus *did* get around to the kid's stocking. Santa Claus sent my baby a full hundred dollars' worth of toys and things to eat and fine baby-clothes. And Santa Claus sent him a savings-bank book too, with fifty dollars in it. And he sent me a winter overcoat and the news that Santa Claus had used his pull with my boss and gotten me a five-dollar raise. And—"

"Good old Santa Claus!" lazily approved Braith. "Some class to the old geezer, after all, hey?"

"Mr. Braith!" broke in the youth with the same explosive impulsiveness, "I've just been to the toy-store and to the provision-shop and to one or two other places that happen to be open to-day, so I could find out who to thank for making my kid such grand gifts and giving me a boost in life and—"

"Tck! Tck! Tck!" clicked Magnus reprovingly. "You shouldn't 'a' done that. Santa don't like to have his mask dynamited off."

"And," pursued Logan, voice a-tremble, "I found out the checks for those things were all signed Magnus Braith. Just as I might 'a' known. Mr. Braith, there isn't anything I can say, to make you know how I feel. But God sure made a *man* when He made you. That kid of mine—"

"Aw, forget it!" grunted Magnus, ill at ease. "I owed you a grudge, anyhow, for spoiling my faith in my feller-man, by paying me back that money. And I wouldn't 'a' known in a thousand years what things to get for a two-year-old kid. So I asked a lady—a Miss Viva Russ—and she helped me out. She enjoyed the fun of it, I bet, even more'n I did. There was another lady who'd 'a' been still cleverer at picking out presents, but she's so busy just now I didn't want to bother her. Merry Christmas, Charlie! And Merry Christmas to the kid. Anything else I can do for you?"

"Yes sir," said Logan, fumbling in his inner coat pocket. "There is. You've been so good to Baby that I thought maybe you might be glad to have a picture of him. A Christmas present from him to you. He's the prettiest baby you ever saw, sir."

As he spoke, he fished out a cabinet photograph, wrapped carefully in a bit of newspaper. Unfolding the paper with much care, he handed the picture to Braith, saying proudly:

"Of course, he's prettier'n that, now. That was taken pretty nearly a year ago. But it's the only one I've got. And I want you should have it."

Magnus, vastly embarrassed, accepted the pasteboard likeness and stared with polite interest on the highly glazed limning of a wide-eyed, scanty-haired, expansively grinning infant. At the bottom of the photograph, Logan had written in violet ink:

> *Charles Logan, Jr. To his best friend*
> *and with his father's service and gratitude.*

Touched by the undesired gift, Braith was loud in his appreciation. And, presently, Logan departed.

Magnus held the photo gingerly between his fingers, wondering where to put it. Just then the telephone rang; and Benson, the Halcyon's manager, summoned him to the theater to discuss some important last matter that had arisen regarding the play. Braith absent-mindedly thrust the photograph for safe-keeping into the inside pocket of his morning coat; and in the press of affairs totally forgot its existence.

He dined with Viva and Maida in the restaurant of the former's apartment-house, that evening. Thence, in his circus-parade car, the three drove to the Halcyon Theater, in the lobby of which Marion Kessel and Dave Rodman were to meet them and to join them in the occupancy of the lower right-hand stage box.

VIVA was unusually quiet. Magnus was boisterous in his glad excitement over the coming ordeal. As for Maida, she was bewitchingly elfin in her alternate buoyant eagerness and pretty fright, as to her adored play's fate.

Turning into a narrow street abutting on Broadway, they saw the Halcyon Theater, nearly a block ahead. Maida leaned feverishly out of the limousine's window.

"Look!" she shrilled, exultant. "Oh, look, *look!* It's there! In electric lights as big as—as grapefruit! 'Ropes of Sand!' Oh, *look!*"

Braith laughed aloud at her excitement. The car slowed almost to a halt as it fell into line in the procession of motors approaching the theater. On the sidewalk the crowd filled the footway to suffocation. An infinite number of faces, shiningly white in the electric flare, seemed to turn toward Braith's car, drawn by the spectacle of a stunningly pretty girl leaning so far out and gesticulating so eagerly.

"I wonder if every one of those people is going to see my play," cried Maida, athrill with the delicious suspense of it all. "And oh, I wonder if I'm going to forget my curtain speech! And I *double*-wonder if I'll get a chance to make it. And—"

A wordless gurgle—something between a cat's snarl and a death-rattle—broke from her in the midst of her gay talk. For one flash of time, she glared into the passing foot-crowd with a face distorted and ash-gray.

Then she shrank back into the innermost depths of the car, cowering low down in one corner, her hands over her eyes, quivering like a lashed dog—that same hideous animal snarl and throaty rattle again and again bursting hysterically through her writhing lips.

EVEN Viva Russ felt the genuineness of the stark emotion that had gripped Maida. Putting an arm about the shaking girl, she strove to quiet her.

"What is it? What in blazes is wrong?" Magnus kept demanding in frantic anxiety. "Are you sick? *What's* happened, little girl?"

The car, though no one noticed it, had lurched to a halt in the crush of traffic.

"It's all—it's nothing at all!" panted Maida brokenly as she fought to regain her smashed self-control. "It's nothing. Just—just what I saw out there on the sidewalk."

Braith thrust his own head and thick shoulders out of the window and glared pavement-ward.

The walk was close-jammed, the conflicting lines of pedestrians jostling one another and moving at a pace a snail would have scorned. Scanning the conglomerate mass, Braith could see nothing to account for Maida's terror. Nobody seemed to be looking at his car, for it was but a drop in the gaudy vehicular current that choked the mid-street.

In the sidewalk throng, Magnus saw a casually familiar face or two. He recognized a few veteran first-nighters—a downtown business-acquaintance, an actress whom "at liberty" hardships had forced to go to the theater on foot, Charlie Logan drifting along homeward on the transverse human tide (snug and prosperous-looking in his new overcoat), a stray panhandler or two, David Rodman, who had left his pocketed car a few doors below and was making his way to the Halcyon by the less slow sidewalk route— nothing thrilling or otherwise likely to strike an onlooker to the heart.

And he turned again, crassly bewildered, to Maida Standish. The girl had marvelous will-power. Already she had recovered herself and was laughing apologetically.

"I'm so ashamed!" she stammered. "I behaved like a baby. But I couldn't help it. Honestly, I couldn't, I never can. I saw such a horrible-looking person—a cripple. The most distorted, awful-looking cripple I ever saw. I never could bear the sight of anyone that's deformed. And to-night, seeing it so suddenly, when I was so gorgeously happy! Oh, I'm very much ashamed! I'm all right, now. Wont you please forgive me?"

She looked in pretty appeal from one to the other of her two companions. Braith's heart went out to her in a great pity. He dully resented Viva Russ' attitude—for midway in Maida's broken explanation and apology, Viva had withdrawn her protecting arm from about the younger woman and had settled back in her former place, her face losing its look of sympathetic concern and hardening into something very like contempt.

"You poor kid, you!" consoled Braith. "It was rotten hard luck. But you don't have to apologize to us for having such a big heart. Most Broadway women could see a cripple going past carrying his head and his legs in a suit-case, without so much as shuddering at him."

"Was the cripple a man or a woman?" asked Viva with uncalled-for sharpness.

"A man—I mean a woman," faltered Maida, adding vaguely: "I—I don't know."

"Don't know?" echoed Viva. "But surely—"

"Don't go bothering the kid with questions," adjured Magnus. "Let her get hold of herself."

"Oh, please don't let's talk about it any longer," pleaded Maida. "I'm just a silly girl, and I suppose I'm overwrought. Sha'n't we forget it? See, I feel all right again now—except that I'm still ashamed of myself."

She held up her gloved right hand to prove her nerves' recovery. The hand was steady as a trade-wind. But an almost noiseless snap revealed that the little ivory fan in her left hand was shattered beyond repair by the convulsive tightening of the fingers that encircled it.

"When I was looking out there, just now," said Braith with a ponderous attempt to shift the subject, "I happened to see a young chap that looked kind of funny in a theater crowd. Now I come to think of it, he was walking home, probably, and not to the theater. He lives over west, a few blocks in the old Hell's Kitchen district. He's a fellow who started out to be a crook, but didn't get far and turned as square as they make 'em. Viva helped me fix his kid up for Christmas. He worships that kid. And the kid's going to be the saving of him. His name is—"

"Oh, here we are!" cried Maida, unhearing, as the car drew in at last at the Halcyon's entrance. "Did you ever see so many people in all your life? And every one of them going to see my play! Oh, I do hope we aren't late!"

Even Braith was not deceived by the pseudo-lightness of her manner. He put it down to heroic desire to appear natural after the mysterious shock of a few minutes earlier.

"Yes," he assented, falling in with her mood, "here we are. And we aren't late. The next three hours will tell the story. I—I wonder if you'll understand *all* the story they'll tell!"

He climbed out of the car and nodded pleasantly to an obsequious liveried giant who held wide the limousine door for him. Then he gave a direction to his chauffeur and turned to help his two companions to the sidewalk.

In the moment when the women were alone together in the car, Viva broke in on the girl's hysterically gay flow of talk by asking with an abruptness that was startling:

"Whom did you see out there? Who was it? Tell me!"

Maida had not time to frame a lie. Her nerves were still wabbly. As a dazed fighter "lets in" a blow to the jaw, she allowed this question to smash

through her weakened guard.

"It was a man. I—I hate him!" she mumbled confusedly. "He was dead. Oh, he *said* he was! I mean, I—"

"Come along, little lady!" boomed Magnus' cordial voice at the door: "We're only just about on time."

CHAPTER X

MAGNUS BRAITH piloted his two charges into the garishly overlighted lobby of the Halcyon. Three out of four of its occupants were as familiarly known to him as are the members of a country church's departing morning congregation, one to another.

The main body of first-nighters was flowing slowly and gabblingly up to the ticket-tearer. But chattering groups were standing here and there, and a score or so of detached or semidetached folk were flattened against the side-walls, awaiting guests or hosts.

A man and a woman—Dave Rodman and Marion Kessel—shook free from a knot of acquaintances and left this wall-supporting coterie, to join Braith. Amid a scattering volley of nods, grins, salutations in varying keys and various lengths, the five made their way through the door and to the lower right-hand stage-box.

The house was full; the lights were up. The orchestra—another Old World relic at the Halcyon—was tuning for the overture. Braith seated the three women and then sat down directly behind Maida.

He was fairly vibrating with excitement. In spite of a subnote of shrillness in her clear voice and the unwonted lack of color in her face, Magnus believed the girl had wholly recovered from her odd little spell of fright. He rejoiced at the belief, for he had been keenly unhappy in his dread lest the shock might mar her rapture in this triumph-evening he had

ordained for her.

"This is the very first real-and-true 'first night' I've ever been to," she was prattling, very fast indeed, "and I'm looking on all those people as if I were a prisoner and they were my judges—or rather, as if I were a solitary writer and they were all editors. After all, it isn't the managers—is it?—who accept or reject a play: it's the first-nighters."

"Not always," Braith corrected her. "And even then, it's really just a dozen or so of the first-nighters that count—the vivisection squad."

"The *what?*"

"The critics. Why, you've broke your pretty fan!"

"I must have sat on it, in the car. Never mind. You spoke about the critics. Are any of them here to-night, do you suppose? Do you know any of them by sight? I wish—"

"Are *any* of 'em here?" he repeated with one of his big laughs. "Why, kid, they're every last one of 'em here. I made sure of that. This is the only opening in town, to-night. See that thick-set chap in a dinner-jacket down there—the one with the short grayish mustache and the high forehead, there in the third row? That's Alan Dale. Alfred Cohen's his real name. The tall, heavy-built chap just behind him is Charles Darnton. Over yonder, one row back, aisle seat, other side, is Klauber. He—"

"B-r-r!" she shuddered. "I feel as if a judge was saying 'Prisoner, look on the jury!' And they are all here to—"

"To see what a dandy play you've written and what a clever kid you are," Braith comforted her. "So don't you go worrying your pretty little fluffy

head over that. See that chap going down the aisle to his seat?—the one with the woman in gray? That's Rolfe."

"Who is Rolfe?"

Again the big laugh, as he answered jocosely:

"Now ask me who are K. & E. and who are Jake and Lee. Rolfe is *The Chronicle's* dramatic man. He is a chap who takes his work of criticism as seriously as he'd take surgery or architecture. He's made a life-study of it, just as a man would for the law or medicine. He spends his spare hours digging up drama-stuff and moiling over it all, till he's reduced criticism to a science. Precious few critics bother to put in all their free nights and vacations studying their profession as he does. That's what's made him the best of 'em all since William Winter. Why, Rolfe has about the most valuable library of old plays in America.. Some of 'em are worth their weight in radium, they're so rare. Plays by all—What's the matter?" he broke off in concern. "Feeling bad again?"

"Why no!" she said fretfully. "Why do you ask?"

"Thought you got white and queer all of a sudden," he explained. "Maybe it was the lights. Maybe it's because I worry such a lot about you on general principles. You look O. K. now. We—"

The orchestra broke off. The lights went down. The base of the yellow-brown curtain glowed golden above the newly illumined footlights. Maida drew a long, quivering breath. Magnus sat forward, his heavy chin combatively thrust forth.

A wave of rustling clothes and whispering voices swept through the darkened auditorium. Then it died away into a dead hush. The curtain was going up.

A FIRST-NIGHT audience in New York is not easy to read. It cannot boo or hiss as do the gallery critics in London. It does not shriek its approval as on the Continent. It is plentifully strewn with loyally plauditory friends of actors, management and author—folk whose friendliness too often leads novices to mistake a failure for a success.

But to the veteran first-nighter there are divers signs not to be misread. Coughing, uneasy foot-shuffling, a covert yawn or two—these mean that the play is in dire straits and can be saved only by some tremendously big scene. Tense stillness during the action and an involuntary outbreak of countless buzzing voices at the instant of the curtain's fall—these speak more eloquently of success than does all the usher-led applause in the universe.

Such a silence, followed by a confused verbal outbreak, at the curtain greeted the first act of "Ropes of Sand." Braith did not even wait for the ensuing hailstorm of handclaps before leaning back in his chair with a grunt of pure satisfaction.

"We've won, kid!" he declared, smiling into Maida's shining eyes. "We've won, hands down. If they swallowed the first act, they'll take a bath in the rest of it. It's going. It's going big, just like I said—I mean 'just as I said.' "

Marion Kessel and Rodman had turned to the girl with much more gushing congratulations than Braith's. Even Viva Russ spoke in kind appreciation. But it was at Magnus alone that Maida looked. It was his brief praise alone that she seemed to hear. There was a light in her big blue eyes he never before had seen in them, a light that filled him with mad hope and madder longing. It was as though all his wonder-dreams were coming true at once. No other woman had looked at Braith in just that way. Yet he knew it meant frank adoration.

How long he stared back into the tenderly worshiping eyes he never knew—perhaps for a century, perhaps for a second. At such moments, time stands still.

It was Viva Russ who broke the spell.

"Pardon me," she interposed, leaning across Maida and speaking directly to Braith, "but you have a dab of powder on your sleeve. I'm afraid I left it there when you helped me out of the car."

For the instant Magnus Braith actually hated the woman who had saved him from continuing to stare at Maida like a bewilderedly love-sick schoolboy—for the benefit of some fourteen hundred spectators. But almost at once he had the grace to be ashamed of himself. And the jarring interruption brought him back, with a rush, to sanity.

He had surprised, in Maida Standish's wonderful eyes, a look that had transported him to paradise. But analyzing it now, as was his habit, he began to see further and more clearly.

"She's crazy happy because I put her play across for her," he told himself. "And just for the minute, she's like a baby with a dandy new doll. The baby wants to kiss the person that gave her the doll, because he's made her so happy. After the newness wears off the doll, the baby'd most likely put up a squall if she was asked to kiss the grubby-faced guy who gave it to her. I'm not going to be swine enough to take advantage of a gratitude-fit. I'm not going to let her be sorry afterward that she thought she cared, when really she was only just thankful. I'm going to stick to the original plan."

With an impatient shake of the big shoulders he settled into his new resolve. Not daring to test that resolve by too fierce a strain, he forced himself to look anywhere—everywhere except at Maida. He even plunged into elephantine repartee with Marion Kessel, who always made him yawn, and upon whom he had precisely the same effect.

The rising of the curtain for the second act came to Braith's relief. He clenched his big hands over one knee and again leaned forward to watch the play. The audience, by this time, was unmistakably and wholeheartedly with the author and her brain-child. Even as an audience that boasts loudly of its sophistication took rapturously to its heart such sweetly unsophisticated gems as "Rosemary," and "The Arcadians," "The Royal Family" and "Peter Pan," so that same audience welcomed with outstretched arms and a delighted grin this new Arcadian play.

From the end of the first act then was no shadow of doubt in Magnus

Braith's mind as to the comedy's success. Yet because he knew Broadway's fickleness he made one last stand for sanity. He would not wait until "Ropes of Sand" had had a run, before asking Maida Standish to be his wife. But he would wait until he had read the next morning's papers for the criticisms. If the critics united, as had the rest of the audience, in acclaiming the play, then he need hesitate no longer. For in that event "Ropes of Sand" was bound to win.

At this point in his reflections a soft little hand was laid upon his clenched fingers. He started violently at the touch. The second act was well under way. Under cover of the box's darkness Maida Standish had taken off her right glove and reached back with her bare hand until her fingers closed about his.

Braith yearned, wildly, to clutch the fragile little hand in both his own, to hold it tight and to kiss its pink palm ten thousand times. It took all his granite will-power to return the loving pressure very lightly indeed and then to bury his own hands in his pockets. He heard Maida catch her breath as though his aloofness hurt her. He felt like a cur.

AFTER the third act Maida went back on the stage under Braith's guidance. The curtain had gone up four times, and the handclaps were still an unbroken roar. Calls of "Author! *Author!*" punctured the volley of applause.

The actors thronged about the girl to congratulate her. Benson, the manager, fairly breathed benedictions upon her with every curve of his wide-mouthed smile. Magnus Braith stood at her side, happier than ever before in all his life. And whenever they could, her dear eyes sought his with that same transfigured glory in their blue depths. Then the leading man took her by the hand and led her out in front of the curtain: leaving her there as he bowed himself out of sight.

The continuous storm of applause swelled to a hurricane. The hurricane fell silent, at a pretty gesture from her. And through the curtain Magnus could hear her fresh young voice, with just a suspicion of tremble in it, thanking everybody for everything.

"I—I don't know quite what to say," she began with a confidingly timid little smile that seemed to warm the whole audience to her. "I hoped I'd be called for, and I made up a speech. It was a very clever speech, too, and I learned it by heart. But—I seem to have forgotten it. So—so—I—oh, *thank* you, *all* of you, for liking my play! Please keep on liking it, won't you? I want you to, so much—because, you see, I wrote it. You've made me ever so happy—so happy that I'm—I'm—I'm afraid I'm going to cry. Thank you!"

She came running back to the stage, pursued by a new whirlwind of applause—applause that now had a personal and gayly affectionate note in it.

"Bully for you, kid!" approved Braith, wringing her hands. "You've got 'em with you for keeps. That scared little spiel of yours went fifty times better than if you'd rehearsed it."

Rehearsed it! She had rehearsed it, even to the helpless little gestures that went with it, a full month ago.

As the curtain fell on the brief fourth act, and the audience began to claw together its belongings, Braith said excitedly:

"Do you see Rolfe? That's a big compliment to you. The morning-paper critics generally chase out long before the end—even before the commuters begin to crawl away. But he's stayed on to the last curtain. I never knew him to do that before. See him sprint out? There'll be a tall swad of swearing in *The Chronicle* composing-room to-night over the lateness of his copy. The make-up man's liable to throw a few fits too."

THE occupants of the box were filing out along the narrow chute toward the lobby. Braith was bringing up the rear. And now Maida had dropped back beside him.

"Listen!" she whispered eagerly, her eyes adance. "Will you do something for me? Will you promise? *Promise!*"

"Will I?" he retorted. "Like a shot I will. You know that. What is it?"

"I feel so happy—so exalted!" she said in the same eager undertone. "I *can't* sit at a table at Rector's with a crowd of people. I *can't*. I want you to—"

"Take you home?"

"Yes—just that. I'll get Viva's aunt or the maid to help me find something in the ice-box for us to eat. And you and I will have a victory supper together there—just we two—to celebrate."

"But I asked those three folks to have supper at Rector's," he argued, sorely tempted. "I can't very well—"

"Yes, you can!" she contradicted. "Oh, *yes*, you can! Don't tell Viva. Just tell Mr. Rodman. Ask him to act as host. I've thought it all out. Let him say Mr. Benson wanted to speak to me about changing a scene in the third act, and that you've waited to bring me along. Then afterward he can say he told them that so as not to spoil the party, and that I was tired and you took me home. I really *am* tired—honestly I am. Please! You promised me, you know. You promised."

"Dave!" called Magnus, his heart aglow.

Rodman turned. Braith spoke a few words to him. Rodman grinned in a way that made Braith yearn to kick him. Then the wine-agent nodded his head and hurried off to catch up with Viva and Marion Kessel.

CHAPTER XI

MAGNUS and the girl lingered behind the others, walking more and more slowly, until at the first of several minor exits they turned out into a slushy alley-walk that debouched into the street nearly a quarter-block above the Halcyon's main entrance. They were giggling like truant school-children at their escape.

Magnus hailed a ramshackle taxicab that hovered vulturelike on the fringe of the theater-traffic. Then he helped Maida into its malodorous maw, gave the address of Viva's flat and followed her. As the taxi swung snortingly and jarringly out of the traffic-stream, he had a fleeting vision of his own circus-parade car at the curb in front of the Halcyon.

He saw Dave Rodman handing the statuesque and flame-cloaked Marion Kessel into the car. Viva was standing beside Rodman, waiting her turn, a crease of worry scarring her level white forehead as she glanced anxiously back toward the lobby.

Braith felt a momentary pang of remorse. For the first time it occurred to him that it was not altogether fair to Viva to make this use of her flat, through subterfuge, and in her absence. Viva was awfully square. He had grown to like her a lot this past two months, in spite of her catty non-appreciation of Maida. Viva always played the game openly and aboveboard. Was he doing the same thing by her?

"Hold on!" he shouted to the driver, rapping hard upon the taxi's front glass as he called.

"What's the matter?" asked Maida. "Have you forgotten something?"

"Yes," he made answer, still pounding to attract the cabby's notice. "I've forgotten something. I've forgotten to play square with Viva. I'm going back to tell her where we're going."

"Nonsense!" sharply objected Maida. "Why, how silly of you! Why should—"

The taxi jounced to a halt, causing a car behind it to stall in an effort to dodge a collision. Instantly traffic began to pile up, and as instantly chauffeurs began to swear.

"What's wrong, chief?" asked the tip-seeker.

"Wait here a second," ordered Braith. "I'm getting out to leave a message. I'll be right back."

To either side of the halted taxi seeped the overflow of dammed traffic. On either side no less than two lines of vehicles barred Magnus' route to the sidewalk. He stood in the street, hesitant and glowering, a storm-center of converging blasphemy.

"Oh, *please* come back!" besought Maida from within the taxi. "Their car is starting off. I can see it. You are too late. You can't catch up with it."

BRAITH reluctantly got back into the taxi.

"I'm sorry" he said simply, adding: "Well, I did all I could. If she's sore on me, she'll have to be—that's all. But I hope she won't be—I like her a lot. I guess we'd better stop at Rector's on the way uptown. I can get out and leave word there for her that we've gone on to her flat."

"If you only want to tell her we are going home," interposed Maida, "I could have saved you all this trouble, in the first place. I supposed you had something else to tell her. She knows I may go straight back to her flat and take you with me for something to eat. I told her I might. I told her so, before dinner, and she said it was all right. Oh, wasn't it *horrible* the way those drivers swore? I didn't know there were so many swear-words in the English language. I'm so glad we're out of the tangle at last. I thought we'd be penned up there till New Year's, at the very least. I haven't half thanked you for the wonderful Christmas presents. Now that I'm going to have money from my play, I'll be able to give presents too. I wish the first royalty-check had come in before Christmas. But I can still give birthday presents. When is your birthday?"

"Mine!" exclaimed Magnus in surprise. "Why, bless your generous little soul. *I* don't know—sometime in the winter, and I'll be thirty-eight: that's all I ever bothered to remember about it. But even if I knew, I wouldn't let a kid like yourself go spending your pennies on me. So forget it!"

"You don't even know when your birthday is!" she rebuked. "I've heard of ever so many careless people, but never before of a man who was so careless he lost his own birthday. You don't deserve to have one, when you don't take any better care of it than that. But I'm going to be nice and open-hearted. I'm going to give you a birthday."

"A *what?*" he asked, puzzled.

"A birthday. Everybody ought to have at least one birthday a year. And if you've lost yours, you must have another. I'm going to give it to you. Let me see—this is December twenty-fifth—commonly known as Christmas. What time is it?"

"Oh, about half-past eleven," he said, trying to catch her drift.

"Good! We'll be sitting down to supper about a minute after twelve. That will make it December twenty-sixth. So your birthday, after this, will be December twenty-sixth. Isn't that a nice date? It's a perfectly lovely date. And you can have it for your birthday. Aren't I generous?"

"You sure are," he assented, belatedly falling in with her nonsense mood. "And December twenty-sixth it shall be, from henceforth and forever. That date shall shine in history and in p'lice-court annals as the birthday of Magnus Braith, Esquire. A grand date it is for anyone who wants to graft birthday presents," he went on with a chuckle, "when every soul on earth is flat broke from buying Christmas things. Nobody'll be able to scrape up enough cash to buy me even a measly card."

"No money will be needed," she explained. "Don't you see? All the people you ever met will be sending you all the Christmas presents they got and don't want. You'll be snowed under."

"With Christmas discards? Thanks, a lot! This is sure some cheery date you've framed up for my birthday. Many happy returns to me!"

"Perhaps," she ventured shyly, "perhaps you may get at least *one* present, this birthday, that won't be a discard."

"What do you mean?"

"A present I'm going to give you."

"Look here, you little girl," he expostulated, "drop that idea and drop it quick. D'you think I'm going to let you blow your good money on presents for a dub like me? Well, I'm not. Besides, you haven't got any cash yet. You told me yourself that every cent of your 'Ropes of Sand' advance went toward the mortgage on your Dad's house. And a dandy thing it was for you to spend it that way too, if anybody should ask you. So where does the cash for presents come in—even if I'd let you do it?"

"The best things," she said dreamily, all the banter gone from her voice, "the very, *very* best things, aren't buyable. They have nothing to do with money—nothing at all."

"But—"

"Here we are!" she broke in as the taxi wheezed to a halt in front of the beehive apartment-house. "I never knew uptown to come so soon before."

CHAPTER XII

MAIDA rang no less than three times at the hall door of Viva Russ' flat. Then, exhuming a key from her opera-bag, she opened the door herself.

"Mrs. Miller must have fallen asleep," she commented as she and Magnus entered the soft-lighted living-room. "And I remember now—Viva let the maid have the night out, to go to a grand ball of the Gentlemen's Sons Association of the Lower East Side. It's a costume-ball, I believe, and the maid told Viva it wouldn't be over till just about seven o'clock in the morning. So Viva told her she'd better take all the rest of the evening off, after it was over, and not bother to come back here until time to get our eight o'clock breakfast. It was silly of me to forget. But I wonder where Mrs. Miller can be. Won't you sit down and smoke a cigar or tell stories to yourself or think about your birthday present or something, till I make a tour of the flat and see where she is? I want to tell her about the play, too. She was awfully interested."

Having delivered herself of this speech, without pausing for breath, Maida betook herself to the hinterland regions of the flat, leaving Braith to his own dazzled thoughts.

Magnus drew out a thick cigar, bit off its end and struck a match. Then he frowned, shook out the match and stuck the coveted cigar back in his waistcoat pocket. For the first time it dawned on him that so dainty a girl as Maida might prefer their tête-à-tête supper unflavored by the rank smell of tobacco. He sat down and at random took a book from the table. It had limp green covers, and it bore the chaste title: "Maxims for Fools." It was apparently a Christmas gift-book, from its newness and its amazing cohorts of uncut leaves.

Magnus thumbed the wide-margined pages at random, reading a stray epigram here and there and trying in vain to make sense of it.

"Highbrow stuff!" he grumbled scornfully; then remembering it behooved him to learn how to appreciate such dreaded culture, for Maida's sake, he struggled on. From page to page his bored eyes roved. Once, half aloud, he read:

> It would be pleasant enough to fall into a woman's arms, if one did not fall into her hands at the same time.

"Now, what sort of sense does that hodgepodge make? The chap who wrote this must have had a fit of rush of words to the pen."

On the next page he found something that even he could understand easily. It ran:

> The half-world is a stagnant puddle, at which fools drink because their thirst is greater than their disgust.

"Sweet-scented litterchoor to leave lying 'round where a young girl like Maida can see it!" he growled in contempt, slamming down the offending brochure. "That's the Broadway of it. No reverence at all for—"

His musings broke off short, and he sat staring.

The dark portières—as on the night of his first visit— were slowly parted. And as then, through the opening in the curtains Maida glided into view.

Yes, and as then, her shimmering hair was unbound, and it cascaded in waves of silken fire to far below her waist, almost to her knees. Around her lissom young body was drawn the same clinging negligee she had then worn. And her bare feet were again thrust into ridiculous little pomponed slippers.

Shyly the glowing blue eyes looked down at Braith from under the misted radiance of the light-kissed hair. A tenderly alluring smile played about the full

red lips. A faintly luminous flush mantled her flowerlike face.

Braith, still dumbly staring as at a vision, got slowly to his feet and took an uncertain step toward her. The pulses in his temples were hammering. Once more swept over him the queer idea that he was dreaming. For perhaps ten seconds the man and the girl faced each other.

"I—I can't find Mrs. Miller anywhere," said Maida at last in pretty confusion. "She must have gone out. We're—why, we're all alone here in the flat, you and I! Viva won't be back till nearly two."

A little clock somewhere in the bedroom behind her broke into a soft cadence of chimes.

"It's twelve o'clock," breathed Maida, still holding him with the glory of her eyes. "Twelve o'clock! It's your birthday, Magnus!"

CHAPTER XIII

STILL Magnus stood there, after that one uncertain forward step, his dilated eyes taking in every atom of her loveliness, his temple-pulse throbbing, his heart missing every third beat, his great fists fierce-clenched at his sides.

And with shy happiness Maida gazed up at him as he loomed high above her. Apart from the wistfully timid look in her great eyes there was nothing to hint at any embarrassment in so starkly unconventional a scene.

Presently, as he stood spell-gripped, she spoke again. "It's your birthday, Magnus," she said, softly, "the birthday I gave you for your very own. When I found Mrs. Miller was away—"

"Maida!" he broke in. The word was almost a cry. It might have meant anything—everything. The girl smiled and drew nearer to the harassed man.

"I remembered that first night in here," she said, "the night when I woke up and heard voices and came in to see if Viva had been able to interest the great Mr. Braith in my play. You—you seemed to like the way I looked then. You never took your eyes off me. The play was started that night. Tonight it's reached the goal. So I thought maybe it might please you if I—"

"Maida!" he cried. "Little girl! You glorious, innocent kid! Don't you know you can't do this kind of thing? Don't you know—"

The big, babylike eyes grew troubled, almost frightened.

"Oh, you're angry at me!" she grieved. "And I thought you'd like it. I was so sure you would! Is it wrong of me to dress like this? Is—"

"You don't understand, little girl!" he replied almost with a groan. "Can't you see, I—"

"It is not wrong!" she declared. "It isn't even unconventional. Don't you remember—that first night—I was horribly embarrassed and I wanted to run back to my own room? And Viva said: 'Come in. Mr. Braith won't mind. In the theater world, a negligee is as conventional as an ulster. It's the *entr'acte* interview costume of every actress.' Don't you remember she said that? And afterward she told me I had been a silly little prude to be embarrassed. Well, if as good a girl and as wise a girl as Viva says it's all right, it is! *Isn't it?*"

STILL he wrestled vainly for words to tell the guileless child that it is one thing to appear before a man in such very extreme negligee when her hostess is present and her chaperon in the adjoining room—and a totally different thing for her to adopt such scanty garb for a midnight interview with him alone in a New York flat.

But the words would not come at the confused call of his strangely thrilled brain. He could find no way of expressing the fact without wounding her or making her think she had unwittingly done something immodest. As readily punish a two-year-old baby for running into a crowded room in a nightgown for its good-night kiss!

Scowling in hopeless perplexity, he gave up the fight.

"Don't bother your little head about it," he bade her clumsily enough. "It's all right. It's *all* right."

"Of course it's all right," she acquiesced, her look of trouble instantly swept away by a musically happy laugh. "Of course it is. And it does please you, just a little bit, doesn't it, to have me look like this?"

"You bet it does!" he declared with fervor. "It makes the hit of my life. Lord, but you look awful pretty, Maida. You're just as pretty as you can be!"

"Every girl is as pretty as she can be, isn't she?" asked Maida, flushing, none the less, under the rough ardor of his praise. "It isn't the fault of most of them if they can't be prettier than they are. Do you like my hair?"

She caught up a shimmering handful of it, as she spoke, and stepping forward, held it up before his eyes. The strands shimmered like sunset glow in his sight; and its faint fragrance crept to his nostrils and his brain. He tried to speak. She saved him the trouble.

"I'm glad you like it," she said. "And I'm glad I'm pretty—for your sake."

They were standing very close together, and she was looking up into his eyes with that same gaze of absolute love which had shocked his soul into paradise earlier in the evening.

Even as Paul fought with the beasts at Ephesus, so did Magnus Braith do mortal warfare with the craving to seize this marvelous sweetheart of his in his mighty arms—to crush her against his breast, to bury her adoringly upturned face in kisses.

THERE has been more than one known instance where a rabid dog has halted in his charge, at command of the peremptory voice which, all his life, he has been wont to obey. Since childhood, Magnus' rude sense of honor had taught him that a man's one unpardonable sin consists in a departure from his pledged word. It was the voice of his own self-pledged word that now rang sharply in his ears. And so Magnus, at memory of his promise to himself, swerved from the goal whither he was plunging.

He had pledged himself to speak no word of love, until the morrow, to this wonder-girl, to whom all his nature so resistlessly urged him. And he could not break his pledged word.

And so, his florid face going bone-white and sickly from his strife for self-mastery, he dropped his half-outstretched arms heavily to his sides and took a step backward.

"What is it?" asked Maida, studying his face with loving anxiety and moving very close to him again in her solicitude, "are you ill, dear? Tell me."

She laid her hand on his arm as she spoke; then she lifted the other hand to his cheek, pressing its warm softness against his flesh. The contact sent a blast of fire through him.

"Why!" she exclaimed. "Your cheek is ice-cold, and it is wet with perspiration. You *are* ill!"

"No!" he managed to deny, his voice harsh as it forced its way through his sanded throat, "I'm all right—just a bit of a headache. Don't worry."

He moved away once more as he spoke, turning uncertainly toward the hall. She followed him.

And now a gust of healthy self-contempt was clearing his overwrought brain of its vapors. He felt he was behaving like a stupid schoolboy. This girl, this innocent little country girl, had thought to please him by acting as his hostess at an impromptu supper here at the flat. She had arrayed herself in a costume she thought he would like. Her solicitude for his health had made her lay a caressing hand on his cheek. It had all been done with the frank ignorance of a clean-bred child.

And on the strength of these trifles, he had been on the point of blurting out the story of his love for her, of taking an unfair advantage of her gratitude, by asking her to be his wife, before she could have even a few hours of time wherein to adjust herself to the evening's triumph, before she could make certain in her own heart whether she loved him or only felt for him an immense gratitude.

He was himself again, now.

"Headache's all gone," he announced. "It was just a twinge of bad nerves, I guess. I've been smoking too much lately."

She lifted her hand once more to his cheek and held it there for a moment.

"Your face isn't cold and damp any more," she told him. "It is fever-hot. I'm so afraid you're ill! Let's sit down over here on the divan till you feel better."

"No," he said hoarsely, "I'm afraid I must go now. It is pretty late."

"Have—have I hurt your feelings or said anything unkind?" she faltered tremulously. "You seem so—so strange, and so—distant! You're not one bit like yourself. Please don't be angry with me about anything, Magnus. I couldn't bear it—from *you*. And tonight, too, when I wanted everything to be so happy for me. I—"

Her voice broke. She turned her head abruptly away and seemed to struggle for composure.

"Oh, I say, don't cry!" begged Magnus, grief-stricken. *"Don't!* Please don't! Lord, but I didn't mean to make you cry."

She was well within the reach of his arms. Yet he dared not so much as stretch out a hand to pet her consolingly on the shoulder.

"You're all wrong about my being angry or offended or anything," he assured her miserably. "I'm not, and you ought to know I'm not. And now I've got to go home, because the headache's coming back."

"I didn't mean to be so silly!" she said, smiling as she turned back to him and winked away her tears. "It was because I've been so excited all evening—and then because everything I had planned has gone so wrong. I thought we'd have such a jolly little supper here together, you and I. But the ice-box is as bare as Organized Charity. And now you're going home, and I'll be left all alone here for nearly two hours till Viva gets back. *Please* don't go!" she coaxed.

"I'm sorry," he said, reluctance making his speech brusque, "but I'll have to go."

"But *why?*" she pleaded, catching his two hands playfully in hers. "Why must you go? We can have such a good time here—just we two—for over an hour yet. Please stay. I'm so lonely and nervous."

"I can't," he said. "I'll explain to you some other time—tomorrow morning, if I can. And speaking of tomorrow morning, I've tipped a newsman to leave a full set of morning papers here at three o'clock, with the night hall-man, in case you want to read what the critics say, before you go to bed. He's to leave another set at my rooms. I'm going to sit up for them."

"You're going to sit alone at your rooms till the papers come!" she accused. "And yet you're going to leave me to sit alone here. Is that fair?"

"Yes," he said slowly, "it's fair. That's why I'm doing it, little girl. Good night."

He turned once more toward the hall. But she slipped in front of him into the living-room doorway, barring his path with outflung arms, her half-shut eyes alight, her head flung back, her breast rising and falling with her rapid breath.

"Wait!" she commanded. "You can't go yet. You've forgotten."

"Forgotten?" he queried.

"Yes," she returned, an odd catch in her breath. "You've forgotten—your birthday present, the present I promised you. Don't you want it? If not, no one else shall ever have it."

"Why, yes," he made answer, in no way catching her drift. "Of course. Sure I do. Only—"

He had no time to say more. The girl took a swift step forward. The next instant she had flung both her arms about the dumfounded man's neck. Her soft hot lips sought and found his. The white arms gave no sign of relaxing their strainingly ardent embrace.

CHAPTER XIV

THEN, before either of them was aware,—before Braith's dazed mind could at all take in the meaning of the impossible thing that had just happened,—some one had come unheard down the short hallway from the flat door. Viva Russ stood in the living-room beside them.

It was Braith who, over Maida's head, first saw Viva. He noted that her face went death-pale and that her dark eyes were fixed, in something like pain, on the two enlaced forms.

Then, on the moment, Viva had regained her self-control.

"Mr. Braith," she said, with ice-bright incisiveness, "I am sorry I was not at home when you called. I came back here at once, as soon as Dave Rodman told me."

Maida darted back from the embrace, at first sound of her hostess' cool voice. Braith, his face turned in dull hopelessness on Viva, did not see the younger woman's expression—which was perhaps just as well, for Maida Standish's dainty flower-face just then bore an aspect that would have done ample credit either to an angry cat or to a striking cobra. She was not good to look upon, in that brief fraction of a second before she regained her wonted poise.

Looking excessively foolish and feeling a million times more so, Magnus stood gazing helplessly. Perhaps there is, somewhere on earth, a man who could have carried off such a situation with some semblance of jauntiness. But most assuredly Magnus Braith was not that man. Momentarily he was stricken speechless and without power of motion.

Viva, alone of the three, just then, seemed to have complete self-possession. She looked calmly from Braith to Maida. Then, noting the latter's costume, she asked:

"Why did you undress?"

Maida shrank and quivered under the question. Her embarrassment stung Magnus to speech.

"She didn't!" he declared wrathfully. "This is the way she was dressed, the night I met her—the night you said it was all right for her to appear like that. She—"

"I see," said Viva with a semblance of apology. "I see. I didn't understand. She was tired out from the evening's excitement. So she put on a negligee and let down her hair. I often do, when I'm tired. But if she is feeling too badly to keep her evening clothes on, when we have a guest, it seems to me she ought to be in bed. You won't mind, will you, if I suggest that we'd all be better for a night's rest? I know I should."

THE hint was far too strong to be ignored: yet it irked Braith to go without saying something to soften that flint-hard look in Viva's eyes. He had never before realized how much her good opinion meant to him. Above all, he must try to save Maida from misconception.

"All right," he assented. "I'll go. But first, I want to clear things up a bit, if you'll let me."

"Really, there is nothing to clear up," said Viva, moving aside as if to let him pass out. "I understand perfectly. Good night."

"Hold on!" he insisted. "I'm not going like this. You've got to listen, Viva, It's only square. When we gave you folks the slip, back there at the Halcyon, I tried to tell you where we were going. I couldn't. Besides,"— suddenly remembering what Maida had said,—"she told you, beforehand, she'd probably bring me back here for a bit of supper, and you told her 'All right!' "

In his blind eagerness he quite missed the glance of startled inquiry shot by Viva at the other woman, and Maida's defiant answering look. Braith blundered on:

"Then we got here, and the maid had gone out, and we found your aunt had lit out somewhere too. So, of course, Maida couldn't let me stay. She had slipped that negligee thing on, before she knew they weren't here. I was just leaving, and I asked Maida for a birthday kiss. It's my birthday, you know. She didn't want to give it to me—naturally, she wouldn't. So I kind of lost hold of myself for a second and caught hold of her, to steal the kiss anyway. It was a rotten thing to do, and I apologized to her. And just then you came in. That's all. I apologize again."

Magnus lied like a gentleman. But a more useless lie was never told; and had Magnus troubled to study Viva's face, instead of making his instant farewell and getting out, he would have known it. As it was, he left the apartment with a fatuous idea that he had wholly cleared Maida and had with much cleverness taken upon himself the total blame.

As Braith slumped through three-inch slush to the subway, he glanced at his watch. At three o'clock, at latest, he might expect his batch of morning papers—the papers whose criticisms would tell him whether or not he should have the right, at once, to tell Maida Standish of his love. Impatiently he longed to set the world's time two hours ahead.

FOR perhaps a half-minute after Magnus Braith left the Russ apartment, neither of its two occupants spoke.

Viva was laying her white-velvet-and-swan's-down opera-cloak over the back of a chair. Maida had picked up—she had given it to Viva as a Christmas present—"Maxims for Fools" from the table and was ostentatiously turning its pages.

It was Viva who spoke first. Pulling her gloves out to smooth their wrinkles, she put them alongside the opera-cloak and, looking for the first time at Maida, asked:

"Well?"

"Well?" returned Maida.

"Dave Rodman didn't tell me you had brought Magnus here, until we were beginning supper at Rector's," went on Viva. "I came home then, as quickly as I could. I am sorry I was so late."

"So late?" queried Maida. "Why, we had scarcely been here fifteen minutes."

"Then," replied Viva, "I got here just fifteen minutes too late."

"I don't understand you," flashed Maida. "What are you trying to imply?"

"Nothing at all. There isn't anything to imply. The story tells itself."

"What story?" demanded Maida. "What do you mean?"

"I mean that I have very willingly offered you the poor hospitality of my home, here; and I still offer it for as long as you may care to stay. But I don't think hospitality need be stretched to cover the scene I walked in upon tonight."

She spoke with perfect coolness and almost impersonally. Maida went scarlet.

"Magnus Braith has explained that, fully," Maida retorted. "He told you all about it. He—"

"Yes," agreed Viva pleasantly, "he lied very conscientiously—but very much like a man who lacks practice. I thought it was fine of him. Didn't you?"

"Lied?" gasped Maida. "Lied? Do you dare to say you didn't believe—"

"I believed everything—that he didn't say," answered Viva, "for example, that you didn't know my aunt and the maid were out. You can't have forgotten that I discharged my maid yesterday, or that Aunt Mary went home for Christmas."

"I—"

"So you knew the flat would be empty—though you didn't tell him so. I believe, too, that it was your suggestion and not his that brought you both here. Magnus Braith would never suggest deserting a party of people he had invited to supper."

"He—"

"I believe," went on the level, unruffled voice, "that he was as much amazed as I was, to see you in that costume—or lack of costume. You changed into it, knowing Aunt Mary and the maid weren't here and that I probably wouldn't be home till two."

"You dare to—"

"I believe," calmly added Viva, "that Magnus started to leave the moment he found no one was here but you and himself, and that you detained him. And I believe—no, I *know*—that it was you, and not he, who offered the kiss. A man doesn't stand with his hands at his sides and his face brick red and astounded, when he kisses a girl. A girl who is kissed against her will— as he says you were—doesn't have her arms clasped around a man's neck, drawing his face down to her. Apart from those trifling errata, I believe his story in every detail. In fact, it was an idea of something of the sort that brought me home in such a hurry—on his account, not yours."

MAIDA had listened, at first with flaming anger and with frequent attempts to interrupt, but later in scornfully martyrlike silence. Now she said very haughtily:

"If you are quite through insulting me, I will say good night and go to my room. I don't suppose I need to say that after to-morrow I can't stay here any longer. I—"

"Maida," said Viva with sudden fierce earnestness of manner, "why do you trouble to act—with *me?* You know as well as I do, that any woman's acting will fool any man, if she does it well enough—as you do. But no woman in the world can act well enough to deceive another woman. All your treatment of Magnus Braith has been a pose. It served its turn. And I am sorry it did—sorrier than I could make you understand or than you would care to understand. For I like him. Frankly, I've grown to like him, of late, better than any other man I ever knew. And he is too good to be fooled like this. But I have no right to warn him, and it isn't any affair of mine. But when you try your clever acting on *me*—why, I resent it as an affront to my intelligence. Suppose we try being honest with each other for a while."

"I always knew you didn't like me," said Maida sullenly. "But I never guessed, till now, that it's because you're in love with Magnus yourself."

Viva's lips compressed, all at once, into a white line. Spots of scarlet flared into her cheeks.

"Yes," she answered in a level, expressionless tone, "yes. I suppose I *am* in love with him—though I never put it into words before, even to myself. I am not ashamed of it. And if it can do no good, at least it can't do anyone any harm. I've known Magnus Braith for three years, off and on. I always had a sort of vague dislike for him, till once, a few months ago, I got a glimpse at the *real* man. If I could save Magnus from unhappiness, I'd gladly give up my right arm or my right eye to do it. But I can't. Nothing I can do will help him. Even if I told him the truth about the misery in store for him, he wouldn't believe me. Well, let that go. I didn't start in to talk about myself, but about you and Magnus. Won't you be honest with me?"

"I don't understand," muttered the girl. "I *am* honest."

"No," quietly contradicted Viva, "you are not. You are playing some game I don't understand. What is it? I ask only because I want to help you. Why did you arrange this visit to the flat, to-night? There was no need for it, as far as I can see. You knew Magnus was hopelessly in love with you. But you know as well as I do, that you don't care a snap for Magnus Braith. Then what is it? Why did you bring him here? And why were you so furious when *I* interrupted you?"

Maida did not answer. The anger had died out of her face, leaving it curiously drawn and haggard. Its stricken look touched Viva. Laying her hand on Maida's arm and speaking with infinite gentleness, she went on:

"You are in great trouble of some sort. Will you let me help?"

"I'm—I'm—Why, how absurd!" stammered Maida.

"You *are*," insisted Viva, still with that same oddly maternal gentleness. "All evening you have been trying to hide it. But all evening you have been sick with fear over something. I could see it as I can see it now. You have been so, ever—ever since you saw that man on the sidewalk. Who was he? What makes you fear him so? Why did the sight of him make you run such a risk as you ran by bringing Magnus here to-night? Who was he?"

Maida jumped to her feet, her face ashen. She shook off Viva's tender clasp, crying out wildly:

"Oh, I wish I were dead! I *wish* I were *dead!*"

Strangled with weeping, she ran blindly down the hall to her own room, slamming and locking the door behind her.

"That isn't acting," mused the bewildered Viva, staring after her. *"That is real!"*

CHAPTER XV

MAGNUS BRAITH went straight to his own suite of rooms at the St. Crœsus. An afterglow of his big Christmas tips bathed his pathway from the hotel's front entrance to the door of his suite with an aureole of bellboy-smiles.

He went to his study, took off his evening coat and substituted for it a disreputable smoking-jacket. He rummaged in a closet himself for this super-comfortable garment. For he kept no valet. He was wont to say, when folk commented on this lack:

"I've gotten at last to the point when I can wear collars that are too high for me and shoes that are too tight for me. But I'll be eternally blasted if I can ever get to the point when I'll let an upstanding grown man put studs in my shirts and lay out my underclothes and fasten my neckties and fill my bath for me. A he-nursemaid is the one thing I swear I won't have—not till I stumble into my second childhood. And then I'll go get board in a nursery."

Again and again, as he smoked one cigar after another, he looked at his watch. Never before had he so starkly yearned for the sight of a morning paper.

Only after a century or so,—to be exact, at just one minute after three A. M.—did those papers come.

Magnus seated himself beside a table and picked up the first paper on the pile. His eye was greeted and gladdened by the headline at the top of the page's first column:

"ROPES OF SAND," AT HALCYON,
SCORES BRILLIANT SUCCESS

Followed four fifths of a column of terse comment, every word of it laudatory.

Braith sighed with pure joy. Then he reached out his hand for the second paper, and his smile changed to a frown of anxiety when he beheld what journal had fallen to his lot, for it was a sheet whose dramatic critic had won his way to fame through a sea of vitriol.

The critic began with a bald statement that he would as soon think of making fun of a Christmas tree as of the play he had just witnessed. There were times, he said, when praise—and praise alone—was the meed for a Broadway comedy. Such times, he added, were unluckily so rare that a man who had rashly tampered with a buzz-saw could count them on the fingers of one hand.

Such a play, however, was "Ropes of Sand," by Maida Standish—"a writer whose chief advantage over most of her successful fellow-playwrights is in the fact that her obscurity all lies behind her, while theirs is more or less close ahead of them." The reviewer, as in duty bound, mentioned that "Ropes of Sand" contained several amateurishly crude scenes and one or two bits of vapid dialogue. But these, oddly enough, he explained, served rather to enhance than to mar the fresh beauty and originality of the whole.

"Yes," concluded the review, "you may go to see 'Ropes of Sand.' And if you come away with a grouch because the footlights again separate you from Arcadia, don't blame me. I've shown you how to spend three hours there. Thanks, Miss Standish. And again—thanks."

"Great!" yelled Magnus. "He was the only one I was really afraid of. That review of his will bring more folks to the theater than twenty thousand dollars' worth of advertising. And not a nasty dig in the whole thing!"

He reached for the third paper. It was *The Chronicle*, the journal over whose dramatic destinies the great Rolfe presided.

Anxiously, for Rolfe was a mighty influence in the theater-going world, Magnus turned to the review.

"Good Lord!" he exclaimed aloud in glee. "He's written two columns on it. Two columns—and more! And they've put a two-column head on it and slapped it in the very middle of the page!"

He settled down to the reading of Rolfe's notice. For three minutes he read, his jubilant face growing blank. Then Braith leaped to his feet.

"The liar!" he shouted, incoherent with rage, "the liar! My poor, sweet little kid, too! This'll kill her. I'll—I'll break every bone in his measly body for it! Yes, and I'll jail him for criminal libel, besides! The liar!"

CHAPTER XVI

ROLFE had evidently written his review in haste in order to catch *The Chronicle's* second edition, for it lacked much of his wonted scholarly polish. But in the story he had to tell, it was the matter, rather than the manner, which counted.

The criticism began in an apparently irrelevant fashion which made it seem rather like a chapter from dramatic annals than the notice of a current play. This form of introduction is a space-gobbling vice usually confined to erudite music-critics. Rolfe, as a rule, was not addicted to it. Magnus read:

"The late Dion Boucicault, in 1841, followed his first dramatic success, 'London Assurance,' with a four-act comedy which he named 'Torn Sails.' Around this now-forgotten comedy has always hung an aura of stage romance. Boucicault (or 'Bourcicault,' as he then called himself) sent 'Torn Sails' to a London manager. This manager, whose name has mercifully been buried with himself, not only rejected 'Torn Sails,' but accompanied his rejection with a letter which ridiculed the luckless comedy.

"So cruelly scathing was the manager's critique that the sensitive Boucicault was literally made ill by it. On his recovery, he recorded in public a mighty vow that the play should never be produced. Those who knew the eccentricities of the charming old fellow were in no way astonished that he should take so odd a method to rebuke the man who had vilified his brain-child.

"As time went on, and as Boucicault's renown waxed brighter, his friends besought him to forget his foolish vow and let the suppressed play see the light. Those whom he permitted to read it declared it was a masterpiece, in many ways his most inspired bit of work. Even the obnoxious manager, yielding to pressure, wrote an abject letter of apology and confessed that his snap judgment had been bred of a bilious attack complicated by an ulcerated tooth. Rival managers made gilt-edged offers for the play.

"To all this Boucicault was obdurate—though what fellow-craftsman can doubt it was a magic balm to his scratched sensibilities? At last, pride of authorship struggling with morbidness, he hit upon a way to save 'Torn

Sails' from total destruction. He had the comedy printed in pamphlet form, at his own expense and for strictly private circulation.

"Learning that he could not have fewer than one hundred of these pamphlets printed, he ordered the hundred. When they were delivered to him, he promptly burned eighty of them and gave most of the remaining twenty to close personal friends. Each gift was conditional upon the recipient's sworn promise not to allow the pamphlet to be copied and to use every possible means to avert the play's stage-production.

"As the copies were given only to persons worthy of trust, the precautions availed. Once, it is true, a West End manager who fell heir to one of the pamphlets hinted that he might some day produce the comedy. But a storm of censure shamed him out of the plan. They were a sentimental and clannish lot, those early Victorian theater-folk, and Boucicault was their idol.

"In course of time, the story of the playwright's queer revenge was all but forgotten. Owners of the pamphlet grew old and died. Most of the play's few copies were thus lost or accidentally destroyed or found their way into the possession of dealers, who did not know their history or value. Probably there are at most not more than five of these pamphlet copies extant to-day. What sentiment at first prevented, oblivion continued to prevent; and 'Torn Sails' was never staged.

"All this is ancient history. For the best part of three quarters of a century, Dion Boucicault's eccentric wish has been respected. Perhaps not ten living persons have read the play. Perhaps not fifty persons were familiar with the story I have just told. But last night nearly fifteen hundred persons witnessed the stage production of 'Torn Sails' at the Halcyon Theater.

"Dion Boucicault's jealously guarded instructions, after a lapse of more than seventy years, have been dragged forth from their lavender-sprinkled cerements and have been desecrated. The so-called 'author' of 'Ropes of Sand' has added to desecration the crime of bald and barefaced theft. In front of the Halcyon curtain last night she blushingly admitted that she herself wrote the play.

"This remarkable purloiner of a dead man's wit and defiler of a dead man's secrets is mentioned on the program as 'Miss Maida Standish.' Press-notices proclaim that 'Ropes of Sand' is her first play. It is not her first play. It is Dion Boucicault's second play.

"Miss Maida Standish has for the most part contented herself with wholesale 'lifting.' Whole scenes, dozens of pages of dialogue, all the main situations, even the names of half the characters, remain precisely as Boucicault wrote them. Here and there, in the course of the action, the gifted and petticoated Jack Shepard has injected stray bits of dialogue and minor scenes on her own account. An entire play, constructed along the line of such dialogue and scenes, would doubtless be very kindly received—as a Commencement Day farce at the Pompton, N. J., Grammar School, if announcement were made, beforehand, that the author was an undergraduate pupil of the school.

"In other words, such additions and changes as Miss Maida Standish has seen fit to make are the work of a totally uninspired and equally unpromising amateur. Because these changes and additions are so few, the strength of the master's play does not suffer from them.

"How or where the fair pilferer managed to get hold of a copy of Boucicault's extremely rare pamphlet is a mystery. But there is no mystery whatever in the fact that not one playgoer in fifty thousand (including my learned fellow-critics) would recognize the theft. Stage history is made rapidly. The dramatic events of thirty years ago are practically forgotten to-day, except when they are brought to mind by one of the misguided all-star spring revivals. The dramatic events of seventy years back are as dead as Cheops, save where the oft-printed word keeps them alive.

"Miss Maida Standish has not committed plagiarism. She has committed grand larceny.

"To the amusingly spectacular Magnus ('White Light') Braith is ascribed the credit of fathering 'Ropes of Sand,' at the Halcyon. His also is the glory of 'discovering' Miss Maida Standish and of spending a truly Braithlike sum on the play's gorgeous production. No one who knows Mr. Braith personally or by repute will be surprised to learn all this.

"Perhaps Mr. Braith himself, in the course of his deep reading, came upon the rare pamphlet. Few chauffeurs or traffic policemen can excel this Broadway notable in scope of erudite reading or in his love of scholarship for scholarship's sake. He has long been a patron of dramatic art. But the present situation throws a startlingly new sidelight on his studious tendencies and on his zest for research."

THE review went on for perhaps a thousand words more in the same generous strain and ended with an expression of the author's willingness to prove in court his statements anent the identity of "Ropes of Sand" with "Torn Sails."

Magnus read every word of the horrible screed—read it, muttering, swearing, mouthing.

The review's stinging gibes concerning himself passed him by, like fly-buzzing. They dwindled to nothingness before the stupendous blasphemy that Rolfe had uttered against Maida Standish.

In public print—to nearly a million people—this man had declared that Braith's divine little sweetheart was a common thief—a thief of the very vilest type, a thief of dead man's brains.

The corded veins bulged on Braith's forehead. His collar had all at once become excruciatingly tight. Bit by bit he forced himself to a less blind but no less raging state of mind. He could not kill outright this defamer of the girl he loved. That would mean police-court notoriety for her and in every way would make her position ten times worse.

No, there was just one thing to do. He must follow his earlier impulse. He must give Rolfe such a thrashing as would in some tiny part avenge his sweetheart's wrongs. He must do it, if possible, in private, and settle out of court any damage claim the victim might bring. Then, in both civil and criminal courts he must sue for libel.

CHAPTER XVII

BRAITH caught up a telephone directory, where he found and jotted down the address he sought. Discarding his house-jacket for the coat and overcoat he had laid aside, he jammed his hat down over his ears and strode to a cane-rack.

There from a dozen sticks he selected with loving care a curio that an actor, returning from Cape Town, had given him. It was a polished black cane of no great diameter, made out of a strip of cured rhinoceros-hide wrapped around a thin and flexible steel bar that ran down the stick-center from handle to ferrule.

The cane was light. It could be bent double, like a tempered sword-blade, but it was unbreakable. And a blow from it would cut through cloth and skin and flesh as readily as through sheets of wet paper. With such a weapon Africanders have flogged tough Kaffirs to death.

Ten minutes later Braith's taxicab halted at the uptown apartment-house where Rolfe had his bachelor quarters. Stamping into the lower hallway, Magnus halted at the switchboard-bench. There he prodded from slumber a snoring mulatto who combined the functions of hall-boy and elevator-president.

"Mr. Rolfe in?" snapped Magnus, bulking big above the blinking youth.

"Yessah—yes," mumbled the rudely aroused sleeper—adding resentfully: "Whaffor you-all go pokin' that stick in ma ribs? Ah ain't no—"

"Is Mr. Rolfe in?" repeated Magnus.

"Sho he's in," grumbled the mulatto. "Wheah-all would he be at fo' o'clock in de mo'nin'? An', Ah don' like nobody to come pirootin' roun' here, pokin' me in de ribs, neither. Ah ain't used to—"

"Here's something else you aren't used to, either," interrupted Braith, taking out a wad of money and flaying a twenty-dollar bill therefrom.

He held the bill in front of the youth, whose blinking eyes forthwith lost their sleepy crossness and beamed upon the oblong of Government paper.

"Call up Mr. Rolfe," ordered Magnus. "Tell him I'm here—Magnus Braith. Say I want to see him upstairs, in his own rooms. If he'll see me, all right. If he won't, I want you to tell me how to get to his front door. And then I want you to go by-by here again till I come down. I'll get in, all right. My shoulder's a good enough key for any of these jerry-built flat doors. Get me?"

AS he spoke, he very neatly tore the twenty-dollar bill in half and laid one of the bill's severed halves on the switchboard desk.

"That's yours," he said. "If I get to see Mr. Rolfe in his rooms, I'll give you the other half when I come down again. You can patch the bill together with plaster, and it will pass anywhere. You know that. If I *don't* get to his rooms—well, that half-bill is nothing but waste-paper to you. I guess you know that too. Now ring him up."

The hope-scourged lad hastily bent his energies to the switchboard. As no reply was at once forthcoming, he turned apologetically to Magnus:

"Ain't ma fault, suh," he protested. "Dat room-phone of his'n is buzzin' a reg'lar Swiss bell-ringah chime. But Ah 'spect he's too deep in de hay to heah it. Ah'll—dah he is, now!" he broke off.

As the mulatto, through the transmitter, announced Mr. Braith's presence, Magnus toyed furtively with the walking-stick.

"He say 'Send 'im up,' sah," presently reported the youth, springing from his bench and preparing to exercise his prowess as elevator-pilot. "Dis way, suh. *If* yo' please."

"He's got nerve, anyhow," mentally vouchsafed Magnus as the cage bore him aloft. "I'll grant him that. He must know what I'm here for."

He got out at an upper floor and rang the bell of a door the worshiping mulatto pointed out. At once the summons was answered. The door swung open. And Rolfe—his tall, lean body wrapped in a gray bath-robe, stood on the threshold.

For an instant neither man spoke. Rolfe's hair was tousled from sleep, but he seemed wholly at his ease. Magnus spoke first, his voice coming from far down his throat and through shut teeth.

"I take it this is a surprise visit," he said.

"No," contradicted Rolfe. "I rather expected you—but not till morning. Come in, if you like."

HE turned and reentered his apartment. Magnus followed, closing the door behind him and putting up the chain. He heard the *pad-pad-pad* of Rolfe's slippered feet going down the dark hallway ahead of him and into a room beyond, and Braith followed.

Rolfe switched on a bunch of lights, revealing a room that seemed to be not only lined with books but piled and stacked with them as well. Magnus Braith had never before seen so many books at one time—except once, when he had visited the Public Library to decide a Knickerbocker-bar wager as to whether or not Daniel Webster were really the author of Webster's Dictionary.

To Braith, books were merely books. At a glance he would have placed the value of the red-and-gold-bound reprint Sheridan set far above that of the mildewed-looking first-edition Congreve volumes locked so carefully in a little wall-cabinet. And to waste so much precious room-space on literature seemed to him ridiculous.

But just now these reflections of his were purely subconscious. All his sentient mind was fixed on the tall, slender man in the gray bath-robe, who was eying him in untroubled curiosity.

From the very force of his wrath, Magnus feared to trust himself to launch upon the theme of his visit until he could gain surer self-command. The sight of Rolfe had fanned hotter the fires in his brain.

"So this visit isn't a surprise to you?" he heard himself saying in a voice that would not stay steady or in its wonted key. "What d'ye mean?"

"I naturally supposed you would read my review in *The Chronicle*," answered Rolfe, pleasantly, "and that you would want an explanation."

"Did, hey?" grated Magnus, lovingly fingering the cane. "Well, you're dead wrong. I don't want any explanation—because there's nothing that can be explained. I don't even want any retraction, though I'll bet ten thousand dollars your paper'll be eager enough to print one."

"Then," asked Rolfe, covering an evidently genuine yawn, "may I ask what you *do* want? It must have been something fairly important—to make you rouse a tired man out of bed at this time of night."

"It's important, all right," sneered Magnus. "Don't you doubt that, for one minute. And as for your being tired, you'll be a whole lot tireder—so tired that a wee restful month at the hospital will be just about your ticket."

"I am sleepy," replied Rolfe, with no emotion at all, "and it's cold. I want to get back to bed. Will you please state your business, Mr. Braith?"

"Yes," rumbled Magnus, lurching slowly forward as he spoke, his eyes smoldering redly, his right fist gripping tighter the cane's fretted handle. "Yes, I'll state my business. I came here for two things: first, to thrash you till I can't lift my arm any longer or till you're too dead to feel it; second, to tell you that my counsel is going to start civil and criminal libel suits, first thing to-morrow morning—against you personally and against your paper. You'll be writing criticisms for the warden up at Sing Sing this time next month, you swine!"

HE advanced another step, the cane poised. To his amazement Rolfe did not flinch or throw himself on guard. Instead, the critic flicked the ash from a cigarette he had lighted and continued to meet his guest's glowering eyes with the same unconcerned expression.

"So far as the thrashing goes," said Rolfe coolly, "that can wait for a minute or so. Perhaps it can wait indefinitely. Who knows? But before we muss up my study with a rough-and-tumble fight, let us touch on the subject of the libel. Mr. Braith, I begin to think I've done you an injustice."

"Apologies won't get you anywhere," snarled Braith, albeit a trifle disconcerted by the other's coolness.

"Yet I wish to tender an apology," pursued Rolfe with painstaking courtesy. "When I wrote that review, I was morally certain you were a knave—certain you knew beforehand that the play was Boucicault's, and that you tried to bamboozle the public. In that belief I wrote about you as I did. Since you have been here to-night, your manner, the way you take all this, has somehow made me change my opinion. I believe you were merely a dupe, and that you went into the matter in blind good faith. That's why I apologize—for writing of you as I did."

"We're not talking about *me*," retorted Magnus unmoved, "but about Miss Standish. Jail and libel costs won't pay in full for the dirty charge you made against her in print. That's where the thrashing comes in. And here's where you're due to get it. A hundred-thousand dollar damage-suit will be your paper's New Year's card from me."

"As I said," repeated Rolfe, unmoved, "the thrashing can wait. As for the libel-suit, that will not be brought."

The quiet positiveness wherewith he spoke bewildered Magnus once more, and again it checked the swing of his half-upraised arm. Whatever might be his ignorance of women, Magnus Braith was most assuredly no fool in his estimate of his fellow-men. And this man nonplused him.

"The libel-suits will not be brought," went on Rolfe, speaking with slow distinctness as though to impress a lesson on a dull-witted child. "No suits will be brought, either against *The Chronicle* or against me—because no libel exists: what I wrote was the simple truth."

"It was a lie—a lie!" flamed Magnus. "You slandered the best, whitest woman God ever made. You lied!"

"We'll let that pass too—for the present," replied Rolfe. "Under the circumstances, I can't resent it. For I begin to see what this means to you. I ought to knock you down, but I feel more like—"

"D'you mean to stick to that?" demanded Magnus, vaguely impressed again by the other's air of sincere pity. "D'you mean to stick to that lie in court—to claim, still, that 'Ropes of Sand' is a steal?"

"The case will not go to court, Mr. Braith. Let us settle it here and now—though, frankly, I'd almost rather take the thrashing than to tear down your ideals—or any man's. You saw 'Ropes of Sand.' As you backed the whole enterprise, you probably read the 'script too, and attended the rehearsals. So, I take it, you are fairly familiar with the play."

"I ought to be," agreed Magnus. "I b'lieve I could spout every line in it, by now. But what's that got to do with—"

"Then," resumed Rolfe, "the rest is easy—pitifully easy. I am going to let you judge the case for yourself. I will abide by your own verdict."

He turned his back on Magnus and crossed the room to one of several wall-cabinets. This he unlocked and took therefrom a handful of thin paper-bound books of varying sizes and hues and in various states of decay. Sorting these, he chose one pamphlet and restored the rest to their place, Magnus watching him dully, the while.

"I picked this up at a secondhand shop in Cheapside, two summers ago," Rolfe said, displaying the booklet he held. "I had read the account of its printing, in one or two works on the early Victorian drama. It was a miracle that the thing fell into my hands, for it's a treasure. I compared it with a copy that is kept under lock and key at the Bodleian Library, and it is genuine."

"What is it?" asked Magnus thickly.

"It is one of the very few extant copies of Dion Boucicault's pamphlet play, 'Torn Sails.' I chanced to be rereading it one night only last month. That is why the dialogue is so fresh in my memory. I am going to let you read this for yourself, Mr. Braith. If you are the man I thought you were before you came here, you will destroy it to prevent me from defending any suit you may bring. If you are the kind of man I am beginning to think you, you will remember it is a treasure and hand it back to me unharmed. In either event, the copy at the Bodleian is available, in case of a suit."

Magnus, in lofty contempt, had already snatched the pamphlet from him and opened it at random. With an elaborate sneer on his lips he glanced along the open page.

Then suddenly he sat down very hard in the nearest chair and opened the little book at its first page.

FOR one hour Magnus Braith did not stir or speak or look up from the book. He was, at best, a slow reader. And now, for many reasons, he was reading more slowly than was his wont. His hat was tilted forward over his eyes. He had not troubled to remove it when he came in.

Rolfe watched him for a minute or two; then he disappeared into his bedroom. When he emerged therefrom, fully dressed, Magnus was still crouched forward, reading, his face starkly blank and empty, like an idiot's.

Rolfe turned on the steam in the radiator, closed a window and seated himself in another chair—whence, leaning back at ease, he covertly watched his visitor.

At last Magnus looked up. And Rolfe, who had been able to see only his half-averted profile, was unspeakably shocked at sight of his full face. It was the visage of a stricken man, infinitely old, torture-racked, ghastly.

"Mr. Braith!" cried Rolfe. Then he paused, uncertain.

Magnus turned his wide, blank stare on the critic, but did not speak. His lips were cracked and discolored, like a fever-patient's.

"Let me get you a drink," urged Rolfe in real concern.

Magnus did not answer, but continued to gape unseeingly at his host. Rolfe repeated the invitation. Braith pulled himself together by visible effort.

"Thanks, no," he said heavily. "I don't use it. Sorry I routed you out of bed. Good night."

He swung heavily about and made for the door of the room. His shoulder struck the doorpost in his blind progress outward, the impact nearly throwing him off his dizzy balance.

Uncertainly, his big body wavering, he reached the outer door of the flat. He fumbled with its catch, wondered stupidly how the chain happened to be on, and with Rolfe's help let himself out onto the landing.

Rolfe rang for the elevator and watched his visitor descend in it, out of sight.

Then, feeling infinitely less jubilant than before, over his success in "beating the town" with the exposure of Maida Standish's fraud, the critic shut the door and returned to his study. His watch told him it was after five o'clock in the morning. Yet he sat down, while the mood was still strong upon him, and wrote a quarter-column statement for the following day's issue of *The Chronicle*.

In this statement he unqualifiedly retracted what he had written on the previous day as to Braith's complicity in Maida's theft. He declared, on his own responsibility, that Magnus had acted in entire good faith throughout the rotten transaction and that his mistake had been one that even the most astute theatrical managers in New York might readily have made. By foreseeing the value of such a play, he added, Mr. Braith had proven his acumen as a judge of the best in dramatic art.

Rolfe felt better after this voluntary penance. He crossed to the table for another cigarette. There he saw Magnus' forgotten cane. He picked it up, eyed it with curiosity and made a tentative cut with it at a leather couch-pillow.

The tough leather of the cushion parted in a deep, clean gash, as if sliced with a razor.

"It's just as well, perhaps," softly mused Rolfe, eying the ruined pillow. "It is just as well, perhaps, that I got him to postpone the thrashing."

CHAPTER XVIII

BRAITH came to himself and looked around him like a newly waked sleep-walker. For nearly two hours he had walked in unseeing and unthinking aimlessness, taking no heed of his surroundings, realizing nothing except that he was in torture and that presently he must try to think.

Slowly, the exercise and the chill air began to lift the pain-fogs from his brain. He saw that the weather had cleared and that a fat red sun was butting its way zenithward over the misty shoulder of a low Long Island hill to the east. The sky was cloudless and blue-white. The slush had frozen on shrub and tree in mantles of diamond-bright ice. The dawn wind was blowing—and blowing chill.

Instead of cañonlike paved streets and miles of house-walls, the man's surroundings were white fields and ice-girt trees. A few ragged sparrows flitted past him. Somewhere a rough-throated rooster crowed.

He had strayed due north, and he was almost at the extreme boundary of Van Cortlandt Park.

In little more than half an hour Magnus was letting himself into his suite at the St. Crœsus. Mechanically he stripped off his bedraggled evening clothes, stood under his daily ice-cold shower-bath (which this morning

felt almost warm), rubbed his body to a pink glow with an armful of the roughest crash towels and proceeded to dress for the business day.

A man of lesser physique might well have expected pneumonia at the very least, as a result of the night's exploits. Magnus expected nothing—which perhaps is why the hours of freezingly wet feet had no ill effect whatever on his iron system.

For the first time since he could remember he ate his breakfast without enjoyment. He even forgot his early-morning cigar. Then, at a quarter after eight, he set out for his office.

In the lobby of the St. Crœsus, as he passed out, he saw several men lounging in big leather chairs, reading the papers and smoking. One, he noticed, was reading *The Chronicle*. Magnus had an asinine impulse to snatch the paper out of his hand and tear it across.

Then he reflected that nearly a million people, this morning, were reading *The Chronicle* and that Maida Standish's shame was an open book to all of them.

Every evening paper in town would pounce upon Rolfe's story. To-morrow it would be printed, briefly or in full, all over America. And there was no power under heaven which could prevent this.

THE shower-bath, warm clothes and breakfast had combined to bring Magnus Braith's mind back to something of its wonted alertness. Again he was able to think—to marshal his facts in a semblance of correct order.

Maida was a thief. She had claimed the authorship of "Ropes of Sand." And "Ropes of Sand" was nothing more nor less than "Torn Sails," minus a few old-time local allusions and plus one or two vapidly unimportant lines.

There could be no question of accidental resemblance or what high-brows call "the long arm of coincidence." It was a straight *steal*—word for word, in nineteen scenes out of twenty. There was no chance of mistake. Her guilt allowed no possible shadow of doubt.

Her father, Magnus knew, was a visionary and crassly impractical old bookworm who spent the bulk of his time in collecting rare volumes that he could not afford and in swelling the size and value of his library—to the neglect of his motherless daughter and often to her actual deprivation.

Maida had told him all this, though in a way that had showed him she did not at all realize her father's selfish negligence. She had told him, too, of her lonely girlhood out there in the North Jersey village, and of the countless long hours she had whiled away by rummaging in her father's library. By reading his remarkable collection of old plays, she said, she had first become imbued with the longing to become a dramatist. Yes—and by reading this Boucicault pamphlet there, she had doubtless found the short cut to her ambition. The pamphlet's preface, Braith recalled, had told the circumstances of the play's suppression.

Maida was a thief! She was a thief who fattened on better folk's brains, who stole from the dead. And she was a fool, as well. For no one but a fool would have risked even so tiny a chance of detection, as had she. History bristles with the idiotic deadliness of the knave-fool's deeds. And such a knave-fool, Magnus now reflected in a sort of dazed horror, was Maida Standish.

He had staked all on her—his love, his faith, his hope, the simple trust of a little child for its deity. And now—

Maida was a thief!

BRAITH wondered why he found himself saying this over and over to himself so often. For each repetition of it was torment to him. Thought became unbearable torture. To deaden it he pulled from his overcoat pocket a few letters the St. Crœsus mail-clerk had handed him on his way out. Several minutes must still elapse before the subway train could reach the downtown station near his office. And the reading of his mail might take at least part of his mind off his grief.

Idly he tore open the first envelope. It contained a delayed Christmas card. So did the second. The third was a tailor's announcement. The fourth was a bill. The fifth envelope bore the postmark of Maida's home village. Frowning, he tore it open. It contained a brief note, written in a scholarly if cramped hand, and was signed "Isaac Standish." Magnus read:

> My dear Mr. Braith:
> Will you permit me to thank you for all your kindness to my daughter? I have meant to write to you, for some time, but have been too busy in cataloguing a new consignment of books.
> Before going to bed on the very night of her arrival in New York,

> my daughter wrote me a line, saying: "The great Mr. Braith called this evening after the theater. He has taken home my play to read." And all her subsequent letters have contained high praise of your goodness to her. Accept my thanks and my heartfelt—

Magnus read no more, but sat gazing foolishly at a condensed-soup advertisement above the opposite seat.

To his dumfounded mind flashed back that afternoon scene in Viva's flat, when he had gone thither in response to Maida's tearful call upon the telephone, when she had told him she could not accept his help because she had that day learned for the first time that he was the notorious Magnus Braith!

Yet according to her own father she had written, on the night before that interview: "The great Magnus Braith called this evening!"

Braith's air-castles were tumbling about his ears now, in masses. Their fall tortured his brain and racked his soul and heart excruciatingly. His love, his faith, had gone out unreservedly to this woman. And—what was she?

Loyalty shouted within him against the judgment his common sense was seeking to render.

"I won't believe it!" he told himself desperately. "I'll go to see her. I'll go to see her, *now!* And—and may God help her to clear herself!"

CHAPTER XIX

THE subway train was drawing into the Fulton-John Station. Magnus debarked and climbed to the street, planning to cross to the east sidewalk of Broadway and there to take an uptown express for Seventy-second Street. In this way he could be at Viva's apartment in less than twenty-five minutes.

He looked at his watch—twenty-eight minutes to nine. If he should go uptown now, he would probably arrive at the flat before Viva's departure.

He did not want to see Viva—at all events, not quite yet. In the sulky resentment which filled him he included her. It was she who—probably in good enough faith—had first sought to interest him in the play. She had introduced him to Maida. She was indirectly if innocently responsible for his trouble.

Later he could school himself to meet her—but not now. Moreover he wanted a clear field for his dreaded talk with Maida. So he decided to wait another half-hour before going to the apartment; and in the interim he walked across to his near-by office to get the business routine of the place started, after the demoralization a holiday always left behind it.

His office-force was due, at work, no later than half-past eight. On this past Yuletide morning, naturally, none of them had appeared, on Magnus' arrival—not even the office-boy, to whom fell the duty of unlocking the outer door at eight-fifteen.

Braith had visual proof of this office functionary's lateness as soon as he stepped out of the elevator; for the corridor door of his suite was fast locked, and in front of it were grouped five young men. Two of the five he recognized at once. And the vocation of the other three he had no difficulty in guessing. All five were reporters for evening papers.

AT sight of Braith stalking gloweringly toward them from the elevator, they bore down on him in glee.

"Good morning, Mr. Braith," hailed the foremost as they approached the sulky man. "You're out early for the morning after Christmas."

Braith nodded glumly.

"Whatcha want?" he grunted.

"Seen *The Chronicle?*" queried another, holding up the paper, with Rolfe's story turned outward.

"Yes," said Braith, "I've seen it."

"Going to sue for libel?" asked a third—a cub of two months' standing.

"No," returned Magnus.

"But why not?" sympathetically asked the first. "If that story isn't true, word for word, it's actionable. We supposed of course you'd want to clear yourself and Miss Standish by suing for—"

"You'll leave Miss Standish's name out of it," growled Braith. "For my own part, I've got nothing to say—nothing at all, not a thing. Good-by."

He put his hand on the knob of the locked office door by way of dismissal, although he well knew he could not get in until the office-boy should appear with the key.

"Hold on!" interposed a reporter with whom Braith had been fairly well acquainted for the past five years. "My paper's always been mighty friendly to you, old man. And we're anxious to print your side of the case. We—"

"You're anxious to get me to say things you can string into a funny story that'll make me more of a mark than ever," contradicted Braith, "and I'm not going to say 'em. This don't concern the public. I got nothing to say. Good-by."

"But Mr. Braith," pleaded one of the others, "all New York is talking about the *Chronicle* story. It's only fair to you, to—"

"To clear out and leave me be," finished Magnus. "Chase!"

"You don't seem to understand, sir," piped up the cub again as the older men fidgeted, nonplused. "You don't seem to understand what a very grave charge has been made. My city editor said to me, as soon as I got to work: 'Go out and find Magnus Braith and see what he has to say. He'll be ripping mad. And you ought to get some good stuff from him. He's always good copy, and—' "

"Shut up!" whisperingly exhorted the reporter nearest him, while another furtively and agonizingly ground his heel into the cub's instep.

"Don't jump him," ordered Braith. "He's just blatting what the rest of you are trying to say, nicer. All of you got the tip to come down here and stir me up into a roar and then write the fool things I'd say. Well, from now on, the dancing bear's on strike. The clown's quit doing his stunts for you garbage-collectors. I'm through feeding raw meat to the an'mals."

After this startling mixture of metaphors Braith shoved his way roughly through the astounded group and stamped back to the elevator. The reporters followed. He heard one of them say something the purport of which he could not catch. Two of the others laughed at the low-pitched words. Braith had a mad desire to turn back and charge the five.

Instead he got into the elevator and was lucky enough to see the pursuing pack of reporters reach the shaft a fraction of a second after the metal door had rolled shut.

DOWN in the street he looked again at his watch. Still only a quarter before nine. He decided to start uptown and to stop off for a minute or two at the Halcyon. Benson would probably be there, as his office was in the theater-building and as he must needs get to work early on the morning after the *première*. The meeting with the manager must be gotten through with sometime. And Braith saw no good in putting off the inevitable.

He found a little knot of loiterers on the all-but-deserted street in front of the Halcyon. The idlers were watching the activities of two overalled laborers, one of whom was busy with a pastebrush and paper the other with a screwdriver.

The man with the pastebrush was spreading blank paper above the three-sheet advertisement of "Ropes of Sand" that hung on panels at either side of the entrance. The wielder of the screwdriver was unfastening from its moorings a black-and-gilt board which announced the play.

"What's the main idea?" Braith heard a lounger ask the man with the screwdriver. "The show didn't open till last night."

"Boss' orders," was the laconic response. "It's canned. I heard him say

so. Some kind of mix-up. The backer got caught on some queer deal or other—I don't know what. Second-night money's being returned."

Magnus made his way toward Benson's office, but in the foyer he came face to face with the man he was looking for. Benson was bustling across the lobby from his office, a typewritten sheet of paper in his hand. At sight of Braith he came to a full stop and snarled fiercely at him:

"I've been trying for half an hour to get you on the wire at your hotel or at your office. I began to think you were in hiding. You ought to be, if you're not. A swell mess you and your crooked outfit let me into!"

MAGNUS blinked. Not a year ago he had put this man on his feet after a financial stumble. For the past three months he had been associated with him almost daily. And Benson's manner toward him had been unbrokenly effusive. Yet now the fellow was speaking as if to a drunken usher.

"Next time you have a crook-game to spring on Broadway," went on the manager savagely, "I'll thank you to pick out some other fall guy instead of me. This has given me a black eye in the theater world that I can't live down in ten years. I ought to have had enough sense to keep my fingers out of it. I always knew you were a dub. All Broadway knows you for a dub and a joke. But I thought you were too bone-headed to be anything but square. The smooth little woman who worked the frame-up with you—"

"Drop it!" adjured Braith, speaking almost tenderly.

"Drop it, hey?" stormed Benson, stung afresh by the interruption and still further emboldened by the big man's meekness. "Drop it? You can lay any bet you like I'll drop it. And you too, you big-mouthed crook! But you're due for a damage-suit from me first—you and the Standish wench too. The simpering little—"

With no show of emotion at all Braith reached out, deftly caught Benson by the nape of the neck, shook the manager's mouthful of obscene epithets into an unintelligibly gobbling gurgle and walked out of the lobby into the street.

As he walked, he continued to hold his right arm very rigidly in front of him. And at the extreme end of that arm his muscular fingers still retained their hold on the neck-nape of the struggling, sputtering manager.

Arrived on the sidewalk, Braith looked weariedly about him for a suitable place to deposit his noxious burden. His eye fell upon the whitewash man's five-gallon bucket of paste. This seemed to him as good a receptacle as any other for what he wished to get rid of. Deftly twisting the gasping Benson upside down, he plunged the manager's head firmly and to full depth in the bucket of oozy white paste. Then, rubbing his own fingers with his handkerchief, he walked away. For the moment he felt better.

"He was too little to beat up," he reflected apologetically, "and *something* had to be done to him. But Lord! I can't stand all Broadway on its head in a paste-pot. And all Broadway will be saying the same kind of things about her that he said. What's the use?"

At the next block he encountered a Tenderloiner with whom he had reluctant nodding acquaintance—a man who had twice "done time" for exceptionally clever confidence games. At sight of Braith now, the ex-convict, instead of passing on with a diffident bob of the head, accosted him with a broad and congratulatory grin.

"Good work, brother!" he approved cordially. "It was framed as slick as anyone would want, and the law couldn't touch you with a ten-foot pole, either. It wasn't your fault that old dodo-bird of a critic blew the gaff. There wasn't one chance in ninety against you. Can't you slip him a slice of the rake-off and get him to say he made a mistake? It's worth trying. Just offer him—"

His words of well-meant advice trailed into offended silence. For Braith had not only ignored his fraternally outstretched hand but had looked clear through him and passed on.

CHAPTER XX

BRAITH did not reach Viva's apartment until nearly half-past nine. He sent up his name and was told that Maida would see him. He learned from the elevator-boy that Viva had gone out fifteen minutes earlier.

Maida herself met him at the door of the flat. Her face was deathly pale, and there were tear-streaks beneath her big, stricken eyes. At sight of her abject misery Magnus' heart softened. She looked so little, so scared, so pitifully wretched! Neither of them spoke as they met.

Before the front door of the apartment was fairly shut behind them, she had broken the moment's silence, crying out despairfully:

"Magnus! *Magnus!* Have you seen that horrible paper? Have you seen it?"

"Yes," he said tersely. "I read it. And I—"

"Oh, I didn't think any man alive could have written such black slanders!" she wailed. "And about a girl that never did him any harm! What could have made him say such hideously untrue things. *Magnus!*" She broke off, catching his hands in both of hers and looking up imploringly into his granite-set face. "Tell me—*tell me* you know there isn't a word of truth in his awful charges against me! Say so, Magnus!"

His newly softened heart hardened to flint. He had hoped against certainty. He had hoped she might confess to the theft and in such a way that he should realize she had not known the enormity of her act. He had even let himself hope she might in some fashion explain away the lie of not having at first known his identity. He had hoped—

But here she was meeting him with fresh lies! And his soul sickened to stone.

"Magnus!" she panted in unbelieving recoil as he did not answer. "Magnus, you don't—you *can't* believe that vile story? Oh, this is the most terrible part of it all! I could have stood everything else—I *did* stand it, because I kept saying to myself: 'He will understand. He will trust me. He will vindicate me! And now—' "

SHE burst into a passion of hysterical weeping.

"Look me in the eyes," he bade her, speaking unsteadily, her tears falling like vitriol on his bare soul. "Look me in the eyes, Maida. Do you mean you wrote that play in good faith—that you believed it was all your own, that you didn't copy it almost word for word, from 'Torn Sails'?"

"Of course I do!" she flashed, righteous indignation sweeping away her tears. "Of course I wrote it in good faith. It was my own—every word of it. And I never even heard of 'Torn Sails,' till I read *The Chronicle* this morning. I never knew there was such a play! *Never!* And to think that you, of all the world, should—should—"

"Don't! *Don't!*" he cried, wincing as at physical pain.

"I'm telling you the Gospel truth!" she affirmed with sudden priest-esslike solemnity. "So help me—"

"Hush!" he shouted, drowning the half-uttered oath, his own voice harsh with dread at the blasphemy. "It's no use, Maida," he went on more controlledly. "It's all up. The game is up. *The Chronicle* has full proof. Early this morning I read the play myself—the 'Torn Sails' play."

"*I* never even heard of the play!" she blazed. "How dare you say such things? Oh, this can't be *you* who is doubting me. I never heard of 'Torn Sails!' Why, even that lying critic himself said there weren't five copies of it extant. Where on earth could *I* have gotten hold of one of them? Magnus, you are hurting me more cruelly than I ever dreamed anyone could. Can't you trust me? Can't you?"

"No," he groaned, "I can't—God help me. I'd give my life to be able to."

"But even if there were an accidental likeness between my play and Boucicault's," she pleaded, weeping afresh at his denial of faith, "don't you see I could never have read the original one?"

"You read it," he answered slowly, "in your father's library. It is a gray-covered paper book with red printing on the front cover."

Watching her keenly, he saw her eyelids crinkle in almost superstitious wonder at his knowledge. And he felt as if he had tricked a sick child. But at once the look was gone, replaced by a stubborn denial.

"I never read it," she declared. "I never heard of it. You say you read a copy this morning. If you really did, you must have seen there can't be more than some chance resemblance to mine. Once you told me Broadway seemed to you a sort of pig-pen. It must be worse than that, when grown men conspire to rob a helpless girl of her play. But I'm not going to be robbed! I am innocent. And the play is going right on, just as if nothing had happened. I worked over it, night and day, for a year. It's my own; it's a success; and I'm not going to be cheated out of my rewards."

"The play," Magnus cut in on her splendid flare of defiance, "is withdrawn."

"With-withdrawn?" she gasped, incredulous, her face sagging.

"It is withdrawn," he repeated. "I have just come from the Halcyon. They're taking down the 'paper,' and Benson has sent word to the press, before now—if he's been able to get the paste out of his eyes and mouth. The Halcyon will be dark tonight."

MAIDA did not speak. Here, as even Magnus could see, was no acting. The girl was smitten as with mortal illness. Magnus watched her in heavy sorrow. At last she faltered piteously:

"Can't you get them to go on with it? The audience liked it so! I'm sure it would pay. This will blow over. Things always do. There have been all sorts of reporters here this morning. I wish now I hadn't refused to see them. I might have made them believe in me and made them tell the public it was all a mistake. Magnus, if only you'll use your influence—"

"Influence?" he echoed gratingly, stung to memory of his own predicament. "Influence, hey? Just at present I have about as much influence on Broadway as a smallpox patient at a beauty-parlor. If this thing has hit *you*, it's put *me* out of business for keeps, as far as the theatrical game is concerned. I couldn't get a crossroads manager to put on any show I was interested in, if I paid all expenses and gave him twenty thousand dollars bonus. To-day I couldn't bribe any house in the tall timber to stage me a small-time vaudeville act for a try-out. I'm dead."

She was eying him broodingly from between her drenched lashes.

"You speak about bribing," she said, hesitating. "Don't you suppose you could pay the man on *The Chronicle* to—to—"

His gesture of quick disgust checked her. And once more she stared at him, wordless. Presently he spoke again, his big voice gentle as a woman's.

"Little girl," he said, "why have you fooled me like this? Why did you pick *me* out, from the very start, as the butt for this game of yours? Why? I had never injured you, or anyone else."

"I don't understand you, one bit," she answered in grieved wonder. "What do you mean?"

"Why did you let me go ahead with this play when you knew it was a fake and when you knew I'd be wrecked if the fake was found out? Why did—"

"The play wasn't a fake. I can't help whether you believe me or not. It's true. And—"

"Why," pursued Braith in the same gentle sadness, "why did you make believe, at first, that you hadn't known I was Magnus Braith?"

"Make believe?" she repeated, her eyes widening. "What do you mean? You know very well I had no idea you were Magnus Braith till Mrs. Miller told me so the day after I met you. Don't you remember my saying then that I couldn't take any help from you because I had been taught by Dad to think you were—"

"Yes, yes," he interposed, "I remember all that. That's why I asked the question. You told me you hadn't known who I was. You *had* known, from the first."

"I had not! You have no right to—"

"You wrote to your father that first night: 'Magnus Braith called this evening.' "

"If Viva has been snooping around my portfolio and then telling you a pack of lies about me—" she blazed.

"She hasn't," denied Magnus. "And she wouldn't. I wish she had. I'm beginning to understand—now that it's too late to do me any good—why she wasn't more chummy with you and gladder to have me come here to see you. But she never peeped a single word against you. That's not her way. It was your father who wrote to me yesterday and said—"

"I might have known!" she snarled in a gust of fury. "I might have known! So *that's* where you got it all! The blabbing old imbecile! After all I've done for him! I might have known he'd tell about that silly pamphlet he was so proud of. But I didn't think he'd—"

An instant too late, she caught herself up and glanced fearfully at Braith. Then, on the moment, the snarlingly vituperative mood was gone. Before Magnus realized it, she was on her knees at his feet, her face buried in her clasped hands.

"Oh, forgive me!" she sobbed. "Forgive me! I didn't mean to! The temptation was too much for me. I—I hated it so, up there in the country, all alone in that ramshackle barn of a house, with nobody but my father.

And his head was always in the clouds or in his books. It wasn't fair! It was crushing all the youth and all the life out of me! And I wanted so to be young—to be happy—to *live!* I came across the play. Dad had bought it for a price big enough to pay all our bills for a month. You've no idea how the tradesmen kept dunning us all the time, up there. He told me it was probably the only copy left. I saw a way to make some money without doing any harm. I honestly didn't see any harm in it. I don't, even yet."

"And—"

"I thought it might get me out of that dreadful atmosphere and out into the real world, where I could breathe and where I could have pretty things like other girls. I didn't see any harm. Neither did Dad. He thought it was a great joke. He said nobody would ever find out. And he promised to give up his share of it to me and not tell anyone, if I'd give him a thousand dollars out of my first royalties. That's where my advance went."

"The swine!" he muttered; but unhearing, she continued her sobbed avowal:

"Then I met you. You seemed to like me, but I wasn't sure. I'd heard so often about people being enthusiastic about plays and then dropping them. You were so big and so gentle and so chivalrous and everything! I thought if I pretended to be afraid to take your help—"

"I see," he made curt reply. "Please don't say any more about it. I made a fool of myself. Being a fool is not on the free list. I know that now. And I—"

"Wait!" she implored. "I don't wonder you're so angry at me. But you can't despise me one half as much as I despised myself from the very minute I stooped to deceive you. You can't know how I hated myself for it. Because," she faltered, "—because you can't know all it grew to mean to me. I got to knowing you. And at last, it meant everything to me. And you trusted me —me, who had deceived you so. Oh, can't you forgive me, Magnus? Can't you pity me? I've paid! I've *paid!*"

HE had lifted her to her feet. It shamed him, past words, that a woman should kneel to him. And now, weeping, shuddering, her head buried in his breast, she finished her confession.

"I do pity you," said Braith miserably. "And I do forgive you—if my forgiveness or pity mean anything to you. It isn't my job to pass judgment on a poor ignorant kid who has been caught in a trap. *Guilty* is such a thundering big word that no one short of God A'mighty has got a right to use it. I guess that's all there is left to say. Good-by."

But she clung to him as he sought to go.

"No!" she protested frantically, her face still in his breast, her arms straining him to her. "No! I can't let you leave me like this. Oh, why are you so cold and harsh to me? You seemed to—to care. And you taught *me* to care—to care more than I care about everything else put together. You've taught me to care so much that I can't feel any shame in saying so. I—I love you!"

To his own boundless amazement, Magnus Braith heard the magic words with no shred of emotion other than of dire embarrassment. And in a flash of self-revelation he knew that his wild infatuation for this sobbing and love-avowing girl was dead—stone dead. How or when it had died he did not know—whether during that hour of revelation at Rolfe's, whether during that long bewildered walk, or whether not until, face to face, she had lied to him to-day and had sought to call God as witness to her lie.

"I love you!" she breathed again. "And I'm all yours—if you want me, dear. I tried to tell you that last night, but you *wouldn't* see. And then Viva came in before I could—"

Her voice was lost again, and she waited, face still hidden, for his rapturous response.

MAGNUS stared in blank despair above her head and across the room. He was facing his bitterest crisis. Duty all at once assumed the guise of a destroying monster. This woman loved him. He had made her love him. By dint of his own all-powerful love he had awakened her to response. True, he could no longer bring himself to care for her, to feel anything but a pitying contempt. Yet to his eyes that made his duty none the less clear. And between set teeth he forced the question:

"Will you marry me?"

Perhaps it was the strangely dead tone wherein he voiced the proposal that made the girl raise her eyes to his—perhaps because this seemed the proper time to bring her face out of its concealment. She stared up at his rigid visage for an instant. Then, her arms still holding him, she whispered:

"You are asking me to *marry* you—after all that has happened?"

"I am asking you to marry me," he agreed steadfastly, adding, in his heart, "*because* of all that has happened."

"I can't marry you, dearest," she said, holding him the closer—and thus missing the momentary glint of relief that leaped into his wretched face. "I can't marry you. I can't marry anybody—yet. I'll explain some other time. But—but, darling,"— her eyes luminous, her warm breath quick and uneven,—"need that make any difference? I am all yours! All—"

"*Ah!*"

It was a cry of genuine pain that broke from him as he shook himself free, his expression vibrant with disgust. She started back a little and stared at him astounded.

"Wasn't it enough," he raged, finding articulate speech with a rush of loathing, "wasn't it enough that you threw me out of my fools' paradise, that you've forever smashed my belief in woman and in heaven itself—that you've made me the laughingstock of my own city, that you've taught me that my 'home' dream of all these years was just a rotten nightmare and that the girl I gave my soul to was a thief? Wasn't all this enough damage for one day, without showing me that you're, that you're—*this?*"

She looked very coolly at him during his fierce-babbled outburst. Then, to his amazement she broke into a silvery little laugh.

"You poor chucklehead!" she exclaimed. "Not even that, eh? Well, I've tried them all. I had you hooked, from the start. It was kindergarten work. Do you know, I came awfully near marrying you, a month or more ago? Well, I did. It's just by the sheerest good luck that I didn't. I decided, you see, to wait till the play came out. I needed you, till then—and all you could do for my play. For a man will do more for his sweetheart than he will do for his wife. I know that, by experience."

THE look of dull wonder in his eyes changed into one of incredulous query.

"Oh, yes," she answered his unspoken question, "by experience, just as I said. I was married, three years ago. I thought the beast was dead. I had every reason to think so—till last night, on the way to the Halcyon. I saw him in the crowd. It frightened me half to death. I thought, at first, he was a ghost. Then I saw I couldn't marry you. And my play was all I had to count on. But when you pointed out Rolfe to me and told me how he is forever digging in old plays—then for the first time I saw there was a chance I might be found out. So I made up my mind to hook you good and fast, anyhow. I'd have done it, too, if Viva hadn't smelled out the plan and come scuttling back here an hour too early."

"Maida!" he stammered, aghast, scarcely crediting his ears.

"Then, to-day," continued the girl, with the born criminal's queer love of brag, "when I found I couldn't bluff you and that the play was taken off—why, there seemed only one hope left. And you can figure out for yourself what straits I was in, to make love to a thick-witted, tobacco-reeking pig. But there's always the good old 'last resort' left. And I'm not going back home dead broke. Juries have a cunning little way of taking a pretty woman's word, and of letting her face decide their verdict instead of waiting for evidence."

"I don't understand you," he said stupidly. "And now I'm going. There is nothing more to say."

"Not much more to say," she assented cheerily, "but plenty more to do. I wonder if I should open that outer door and shriek frantically for help and perhaps tear the sleeve out of my dress—I wonder how much I could collect from you to settle the case out of court."

"The—badger-game!" he muttered.

"I'm told that is the vulgar name for it," she said pleasantly. "And it has saved many a poor working-girl from having to slave all her days for a pittance. I like to think I shall go home with enough to keep the wolf from the door."

She started toward the hall. He threw out a detaining hand toward her.

"Let me go, you—you brute!" she screamed, eluding his grasp. Rushing to the front door of the apartment, she flung it wide.

CHAPTER XXI

ON the threshold, his hand reaching out for the electric button of the bell, stood a man. At sight of him Maida Standish recoiled to a halt, the unuttered shriek still holding her mouth grotesquely wide. She took an uncertain step backward, then another. The man, without speaking, closed the door behind him and followed her, step by step.

Losing the remaining fragments of her nerve all at once, Maida wheeled and darted back panic-stricken into the doorway of the living-room. There she collided with the stupefied Braith.

In nightmares nothing surprises us. We are frightened or benumbed, according to our nature, when the three-headed elephant charges down upon us, or when the bed fills with writhing and hissing snakes, or when we find ourselves strolling, totally unclad, on some crowded street. In the dream the hideous situation seems perfectly logical, and we accept it as

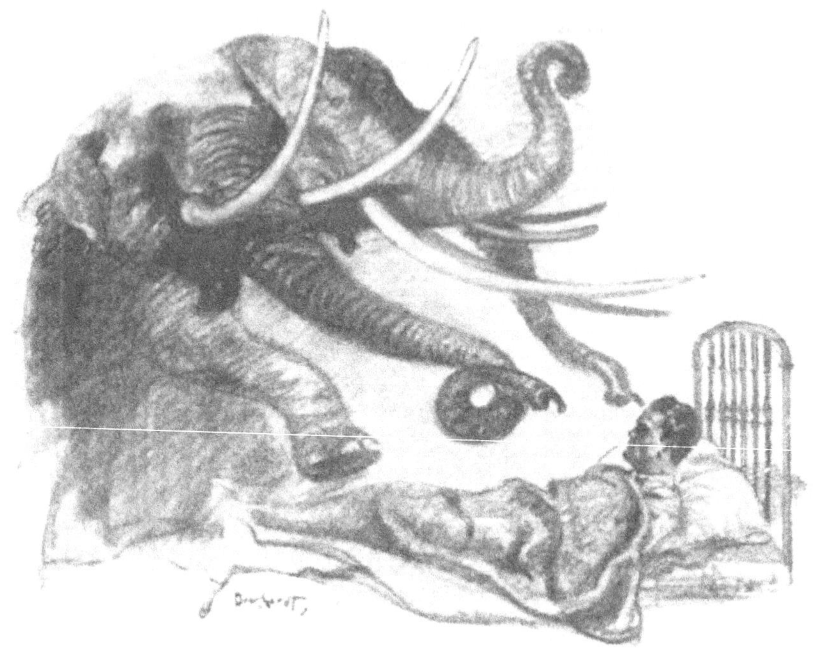

such.

It was the same now with Magnus.

The succession of ever-increasing shocks had at last left him stolidly powerless to feel further emotion. Even as a cup of coffee can hold only a certain quantity of sugar in solution, so nature can contain only just so much in the way of sensation. After that comes apathy. (Witness, the child surfeited with Christmas toys, or the woman who listens to her tenth proposal.)

Magnus Braith, for the instant, was emotionally bankrupt. Had a cohort of angels soared in through the window to his rescue, had a squad of police tramped into the room at Maida's heels to drag him to jail, he would have greeted the phenomenon with heavy dearth of interest. Hence it was with no excitement or curiosity whatever that he now recognized the intruder as Charlie Logan.

Shrinking from her involuntary impact with Braith, the girl had backed against a post of the living-room door. She stood there at bay, her gaze still wide and glassy as it met the advancing Logan's.

A YARD or so away from her Logan came to a halt. He had no eyes except for the cowering woman before him. His glance did not stray to the little living-room near the doorway of which stood Braith, in plain sight.

"They wouldn't let me up here," said Logan, at last. "They said you'd left word you weren't to be disturbed. So I watched my chance and walked up—service stairway. Were you expecting me, that you left word you weren't to be disturbed?"

She did not speak, but gaped grotesquely at him. Logan frowned. Something like a sneer twisted his thin lips.

"Well," he queried, "haven't you got anything to say, after all this time?"

"Blaine wrote to me you were dead!" she croaked suddenly, her voice harsh and shaky. "He wrote you were dead. He wrote you drowned yourself when—when Baby died."

"He wrote what I told him to write," said Logan. "And I had him write it, because I wanted to make you suffer. I wanted to make you suffer a little bit of what you'd made me suffer when you lit out and left the kid and me to shift for ourselves."

"It was like you!" she snapped in a brief sputter of wrath. "I might have known it wasn't true. It was like you to try to punish me. But I'm glad you did it. If you hadn't, I'd have come back. I'd only been gone three days when Blaine wrote that. And I was getting ready to come back."

"Back to your loving husband, hey?" scoffed Logan, unbelieving.

"No," she denied sharply, "I never loved you, from the beginning. I was unhappy and lonesome at home. And I thought you had money. You always boasted you had. That was why I ran away to marry you. Then when your petty little twenty-seven hundred was gone—"

"You went too," supplemented Logan. "You said all that in the note you left for me when you went. Yet here you say, now, you were just coming back to me! You never *could* tell the truth."

"I wasn't coming back to *you,*" she corrected. "I was coming back to Baby. If I'd known how I was going to miss him, always, I'd have stayed on, even if I'd had to put up with you too. But when Blaine wrote that Baby was dead—why, what was the use? I decided to forget the whole thing. Dad was willing to let me stay. And nobody else knew anything, except that I had been away a year at school. What do you want of me, now you've found me? Haven't you spoiled my life enough?"

"Maybe about a fiftieth as much as you've spoiled mine," assented Logan "—maybe less than that. Let it go. I haven't hunted you up because I want you, but because I want to help somebody else."

"What are you getting at?"

"Last night I saw you get out of a car at the Halcyon Theater—with Mr. Magnus Braith. I waited outside till after the show, but I couldn't see you come out. I looked in the directory, but your name wasn't there. At the theater I saw your name printed, but they wouldn't give me your address; thought I was a crank or a masher. I read a thing in *The Evening World,* an hour ago; so I came up here. It's an article about your stealing some one else's play. And in one place it says a reporter for the paper called on you at this address and you wouldn't see him. So I came up. I came to see you about Mr. Braith. I want you to leave him be. He's too good for the like of you to hurt."

"I—"

"Don't lie! I wasn't close enough to speak to either of you when you got out of the car at the theater last night, but I saw the way he looked at you. And it told me all I needed to know. You're trying to make a fool of him, like you made of me. And I won't have it. I owe everything to that man. And I'm going to pay back part of it by steering you away from him. Understand me? I'll come pretty close to squaring the whole debt to him if I—"

Magnus stepped forward. Becoming aware for the first time that a third person was within hearing, Logan swung about to face him.

"Mr. Braith!" he said confusedly.

"Hello, Charlie," was Magnus' rueful answer. "I'm glad you came when you did—not for the reason you may think I'm glad, but because I want a witness for something I've got to say before I get out of here."

"Oh," spoke up Maida with calm assurance, "you aren't going yet, Magnus. And a witness is a good deal more valuable to me, at this minute, than to you. Whatever else Charlie Logan may be, he is a *man.* And he's still my husband. Listen to me, Charlie! I want to tell you what you have just saved me from."

CHAPTER XXII

BOTH men looked at her without the remotest show of understanding. Rapidly, viciously, she began to speak—fairly spitting forth her accusations.

Braith listened with no attempt to interrupt. His heart was dead within him; nothing mattered now; no new manifestation of her real character could further debase in his eyes this woman he had adored. No threat nor peril could add to his own sick misery of disillusion or stir him to fear.

Logan heard her through—to a certain point in her narrative; then, with tired disgust, he interrupted:

"Are you expecting me to believe a word of that stuff you're saying?

Because, if you are, you can save your breath. It's a lie, clear down to the ground. I'd know that, even if I didn't know Mr. Braith for the whitest man God ever yet bothered to make. I'd know it's a lie, just because I know *you!* A man doesn't risk prison to take by force a thing that is his for the asking. And unless you've changed since my day, any man with Mr. Braith's money—"

"You don't believe it?" she asked carelessly. "Well, I didn't really think you would. And it doesn't much matter whether you do or not. A jury will. And you'll have to testify that I told you and that you weren't man enough to resent it. It'll put you in a nice light. Any jury—"

"Jury?" he echoed. "What—"

"I'm going to carry this into court," she explained patiently, "unless—unless—"

"Unless Mr. Braith will stand for being blackmailed for a thumping big sum?" hazarded Logan, the contempt in his face and voice deepening. "And you're counting on being able to scare him into doing just that? If he has backbone enough to refuse, you'll pay him by bringing suit and wrecking him for keeps? I get the idea. Any woman can make such a charge against any man, and his own best friends will believe it—no matter if there isn't a scrap of evidence and if, by some miracle, the jury has sense enough not to convict; the man's damned forever, so far as this world goes. I know enough from the newspapers to know that. It's the one kind of charge that doesn't need any proof—that and breach-of-promise. Either one will set everybody gabbling 'Guilty!' without stopping to ask for evidence. And *that's* what you're framing up on Mr. Braith?"

She smiled approvingly.

"You could always talk well, Charlie," she commended, "when you were stirred up. That was what interested me in you, first, when you came up home on vacation that summer. Do you remember the night I met you at the Guild Hall charity hop? If you'd talked less well—and if you hadn't made me think your father'd been a rich man, instead of an East Side plumber with only twenty-seven hundred to leave you—why, I'd have saved myself lots of trouble."

"Answer me, yes or no," he demanded, his pasty face greenish, his small eyes aglow. "Are you holding that threat over Mr. Braith, to make him give you money you haven't earned? Yes or no?"

"Charlie," she retorted, "I've tried to make it plain, haven't I?"

He looked broodingly at her, the smolder in his eyes deepening, the eyes themselves contracting to mere slits. Braith had an absurd impression of being a mere spectator at some domestic drama, badly acted and worse staged. Presently Logan spoke—very slowly, but with a drawling fatality in his weak voice:

"When a woman of your sort cuts loose against s'ciety," he said, "there's no law to stop you—because a pretty woman can make a fool of the law. And when your kind of woman gets started, the law is 'off' on her, just the same as on any other kind of snake. There's only one thing to do with her—with *you: you need killing.*"

HIS gruesome speech was at odd variance with his own puny form and personality, but in his tone rang a queer sincerity that was all but fanatical. Thus might the consumptive Richelieu have lisped the death-order against Egmont and Horn. Thus might the dying Marat have consigned a new batch of aristocrats to the guillotine. Thus, too, might the enfeebled old Torquemada have whispered his grim dictum: "Kill! And thus let the Lord find out His own!"

Braith was aware of a prickling at his hair-roots as he heard. Even Maida lost a fraction of her triumphant self-confidence.

"We aren't living in the Middle Ages!" she sneered.

But there was a tremor in her scoffing reply. And Logan repeated with the same anemic deadliness in his slow voice:

"You need killing, Maida. It's the only way out. It'll be a blessing and not a curse on the man who does it. Maida, I am going to kill you."

He spoke with a cold fervor, his slitted eyes gripping hers, his white lips twisting grotesquely at the corners.

"Logan!" broke out Magnus, finding speech and sense under the spur of this counter-shock. "You're crazy, man—stark crazy! That's no way for a white man to speak. Cut it out!"

Logan, in the tense concentration of his fanatic idea, did not even hear him. His ophidian eyes still holding Maida's, he shifted his lean body nearer to the now cowering woman and spoke again.

"They'll send me to the chair—though they ought to pension me. But I'm sick of the game, and I'll be glad for a rest. Mr. Braith will look out for the kid, I know—better than I could. I'm wiping out a long score, Maida. And—"

He had ever been shifting imperceptibly toward her as he droned out his strange speech, his bony fingers closing and opening. Now, of a sudden, his hands were advanced clawingly toward her soft throat.

The woman screamed hoarsely and recoiled against the wall just behind her, the fanatic's eyes so holding her that she could not turn and flee.

The long, clammy fingers actually touched the pulsing warmth of her throat.

Then Logan went spinning eccentrically backward across the room, upsetting a chair and striking against the farther wall with a force that knocked the breath out of his body.

BRAITH, all alive again now, towered between the would-be slayer and the girl.

"I told you to cut it out!" growled Magnus. "If you make another rotten move like that, I'll trundle you out of here by the nape of the neck and turn you over to the first cop I meet. Good Lord, man! I b'lieve you'd have done it! You'd really have killed her if I hadn't been here to—"

Maida's laugh (hysterical but still highly creditable under the circumstances) broke on Braith's shuddering words. Hers was a gallant soul!

"Oh, no, he wouldn't!" she gibed. "Don't look so horrified, Magnus. He wouldn't have killed me. He hasn't the nerve to kill a fly—or to kill himself, which comes to the same thing. It was all a bluff!"

She laughed again fearlessly as she glanced across in derision at the man from whom she had just been rescued.

Logan still leaned against the wall, gaspingly fighting to get back the breath that had been knocked out of him. His face was ghastly, and it glistened with cold sweat. Fanatic fires still smoldered behind his bulging eyes. His whole lanky body shook as with violent ague.

"See!" she accused snarlingly, pointing at the abject figure. "He hasn't the strength or the nerve to kill anyone. It was all a bluff. I knew that, from the second he said you would look after Baby. That proves it. Because Baby died—two days after I went away. Died of summer complaint. And I wasn't there to take care of him, God forgive me! Blaine wrote me about it in that letter of his. I wouldn't have believed him, but Mrs. Harding, the woman who lived across the hall from us, had written to me about it the day before I got Blaine's letter. She—she sent me a pair of Baby's socks, a pair I had knitted for him, and she told me all about it. I was getting ready to come back when his letter came. I had found I couldn't stay away from Baby. I found it out before I had been away two days. I had thought I could, but I couldn't. I loved him so. He was the only thing I ever was able to love, and he died—because I wasn't there. I'd have put up with this man for the rest of my life, to be with Baby. There isn't anything that could give better proof how much I loved Baby."

In the quick reaction from mortal danger, her nerves were racing. And—a common phenomenon in hysteria cases—they had led her to a gush of garrulity on a theme that ordinarily she kept locked close in her heart. Now, vaguely realizing this, she returned to the point.

"Yet you heard him say *you* would look after Baby," she stormed. "That proves what a cheap bluff all his threat was. He even dragged in the name of his own child who died—"

"Mrs. Harding wrote what I told her to write—same as Blaine," panted Logan, still shaky and scant of breath. "She—"

"It's a lie!" challenged Maida. "She sent me his little socks, his pair—"

With a motion of his hand, Braith checked her. Feeling in the inner pocket of his coat, he drew forth an oblong of glazed pasteboard—the photograph he had thrust there for safekeeping on Christmas morning and the existence of which he had wholly forgotten in the stress of the past twenty-four hours.

Silently he handed her the picture—the likeness of the scant-haired, large-faced, laughing baby, the photograph across which the giver had scrawled so laboriously, in violet ink, the legend: *"Charles Logan, Jr. To His Best Friend and with his Father's Service and Gratitude."*

She glanced with careless impatience at the proffered card. Then, at nearer sight of it, she snatched the photograph from Magnus. Grasping it tightly in both hands, she stared dumbly, greedily, at the picture's face. Then she sank down upon a corner of the couch, her strength failing, and still with wide eyes devoured the cheap bit of photography. Her lips moved wordlessly, from time to time. But never did she shift her rapt gaze from the picture.

The two men stood uncomfortably, looking at her. Neither spoke; and still the woman crouched there, her lips moving, her eyes strained upon the ill-posed photograph.

At last Braith noted that Maida's fever-bright eyes were dimmed, and that tears were welling up in their blue depths. A tear splashed from her cheek to the glazed surface of the picture. This seemed to break, in a measure, the spell which had held her. From the ever-moving lips issued the crooning whisper:

"My little son! Mother's little, *little* son!"

Braith felt a lump in his own throat. Tamely he said:

"He's happy, and he's well. I guess his father has taken pretty fine care of him, all right. He has lots of—lots of nice things to play with and wear and—"

" 'Charles Logan, Junior!' " she read aloud, for the first time noting the written words under the picture. " 'Charles Logan, Junior. To his best friend and with his father's service and gratitude.' "

She looked up wonderingly, an unspoken question in her wet eyes.

CHAPTER XXIII

"YOU can have the photo if you like," volunteered Magnus, ill at ease. "Charlie gave it to me yesterday—for a Christmas present. He said it was the only copy of it he had. But I guess you're the one to have it. You're welcome to it. I'm glad I've been able to do even a little bit for the kid."

She was looking at him with an expression he could not read. In a moment she said, pointing to the inscription:

"Is it *you* that he calls Baby's 'best friend'?"

"Oh," said Braith, embarrassed, "that don't mean anything. It's just his way of—"

"No!" broke in Logan with sudden vehemence, "no, it *don't* mean anything, Maida. It only means that if it hadn't been for Mr. Braith's whiteness, I'd have been in jail to-day, and the kid would have been in an orphan asylum or the Gerry S'ciety's institootion. That's all it means. It means that Mr. Braith fixed it so I could have the kid with me and feed him and clothe him and keep him warm. And it means he sent him hundreds of dollars' worth of pretty things to wear, and toys and such-like, for Christmas. And he got me a raise of pay, so the kid could have a nicer home and more 'tention. That's all it means. That's all Mr. Braith has done for my kid. He's just kept the kid out of an asylum and made him happy and comf'table and given him a chance in life."

"Mr. Braith!" panted Maida. "You have—you have—"

"And," added Logan, "in reward for all he's done for the kid, you're going to bleed him for hush-money or else disgrace him in public. D'you wonder I said you needed killing? I still say it. And you're—"

"Shut up, Charlie!" ordered Braith.

The girl had thrown herself heavily upon the floor, face downward, the baby's photograph crushed tight to her lips, her slender body racked with sobs.

Here was no acting. Leaning over the convulsed woman, Braith said gently:

"Whatever you decide to do to me, the kid is going to be looked out for—always. You've got my word for that, Maida. And—and I'm sorry I've made you cry again," he ended awkwardly.

A momentary checking of the sobs that now broke out afresh was the only sign she gave that she had heard the crude effort at consolation. Logan took a step forward and seemed about to speak. But Braith caught his arm and by main strength led the half-crazed husband out of the apartment.

"We don't belong in there, just now," he said at the outer hall as Logan made as though to wrench free and return. "Leave her alone. When—when God lays His hand on a woman, I guess it's time for man to keep his own hands off. Come along."

THROUGH the hell of her agony, as she lay writhing there alone, Maida became subconsciously aware that the telephone-bell was ringing—that it had been ringing, unheeded by any of them—off and on for the past ten minutes.

She lifted herself from the floor, struggled to her feet and, waveringly, made her way to the instrument.

Through the receiver came a thoroughly cross voice.

"Hello!" it fumed. "Miss Russ' apartment? This is the superintendent of the building. Been trying to get you for a quarter of an hour or more. The folks in the apartment below you and the fam'ly next door have been complaining to me about the racket. They say if there's any more screaming or yelling or bumping or throwing furniture, they'll cancel their lease. Of course, we don't want to squelch any innocent skylarking, the morning after Christmas. We like our tenants to have a good time, but they don't have to disturb the whole building. The roughhouse has got to stop."

"I am sorry," answered Maida dully. "And—there won't be any more noise. I promise."

She hung up the receiver and turned back into the room. The tempest was past, leaving behind it the awful peace of desolation.

"There won't be any more noise," she heard herself murmur; and into her mind came fantastically the death-speech of *Hamlet:*

"The rest is silence!"

She sat down, holding her baby's likeness again before her tortured eyes. Long she sat there. Then, going into Viva's bedroom, she found a medicine-kit and rummaged through it.

At last she found what she sought: a vial part full of quarter-grain sulphate of morphia tablets. She counted out the sharp-edged little cylinders into her palm. There were exactly thirteen of them. The coincidence of the number struck her.

Returning the medicine-case to its shelf, she came back into the living-room, laid the thirteen morphia tablets carefully in a little heap on the table-edge and tossed the empty vial out the window. Then she sat down and scribbled in pencil on a stray half-sheet of paper the following note:

Dear Viva:

My head aches so badly that I am going to take some morphia for it. Ordinary headache powders don't seem to help it at all. Morphia always relieves me. I brought a few tablets of it from home in my trunk. I'll take one of these and then lie down for a while. So please don't wake me when you come in. A good long sleep will make me all well. I write this, so you won't disturb me till I wake of my own accord.

P. S. Magnus Braith called this morning. He has just gone. He is not in love with me. I know that now. And it is only right that you should know it.

She pinned the note to a chair-back and set the chair directly in front of the living-room door.

Then, very carefully, she gathered up the thirteen tablets and carried them into her own room.

CHAPTER XXIV

BRAITH, the odd sense of unreality still upon him, went back to his office. The world may turn upside down; hearts may break; teeth may ulcerate; women may prove false or uncomfortably faithful; ideals may crash into the dust—but office-work is always waiting, always clamoring to be done. Where our sentimental ancestors pined away from grief, their more matter-of-fact descendants stolidly go back to the office.

Braith entered the private room of his downtown suite by a rear door, so as to dodge any possible reporters who might be lurking in a hall or anteroom. Changing into his working-coat, he rang for his stenographer. Instead, the office-boy answered the summons.

"Miss Condit phoned she was ill, sir," reported the youth. "She'll try to be down to-morrow. And there's a lady been waiting outside here for you, for half an hour or more. I told her you never see vis'tors till two o'clock. But she asked me to bring you her card when you got here."

He laid a card on Braith's desk, as he spoke, thus earning to the best of his immature ability the fifty-cent tip he had received for the service. The card was Viva Russ'. Magnus' thick brows contracted as he read the name, and his teeth set hard. Then, with visible effort, he said:

"Send her in."

Viva, ushered into the sanctum, was shocked at her first glimpse of Braith's face. It was the visage of an old and sick man.

"I read it on the way downtown," she said simply. "And I came straight here. I don't know whether Maida has seen it or not. She had all the papers."

She paused, finding it hard to take her mind from the stricken face before her.

"Don't!" she begged impulsively. "Don't take it like that. I can't bear to see you look so! You mustn't let it strike so deep. I know all it must mean to you. But—"

"It doesn't mean anything to me," he denied drearily. "Nothing does. It's all finished."

"But you must hear Maida's side of the story, before you say that!" she pleaded. "Perhaps, after all, there's a mistake. Don't judge her too harshly. Perhaps she—"

"I'm not judging her at all," came the answer in that same drearily apathetic voice. "I've seen her. And there's no mistake."

"You've seen her?"

"I just came from there."

"She didn't even deny—"

"Not after a while. At first, she did, of course. She would. But she owned up afterward. The whole thing was a steal. She needed the money, and she wanted to get away from where she lived and get some fun out of life. She thought no one would know. Her swine of a father was in it too."

THERE was a silence. And then: "What are you going to do?" she asked.

"Do?" he repeated heavily. "Why, there's nothing left to do. Everything's done. The show's withdrawn. The reporters are yapping at my heels. Folks are pretty unanimous in agreeing I'm a crook. Maida's told me the truth about myself, at last. I wouldn't have minded all that, so much—only she's told the truth about *her*self too. That's where the real hell comes in. Yes, everything's 'done,' all right, all right."

"What do you mean when you say she 'told the truth about herself?' "

"That she'd never cared for me—that she'd played me for a sucker from the very start, that she means to blackmail me into giving her enough cash to keep her comf'table for life. That and a few other little things!"

"Oh, you must be wrong!" cried Viva. "You *must!* You must have misunderstood her. She never could have said—"

"If she hadn't said it all, plain as print," he rejoined, "a bone-head like me wouldn't have understood or believed it. Oh, it's true, all right. I might have known, months ago, that I was walking in my sleep. I might have known there wasn't really any girl alive like the wonder-girl I'd been fool enough to dream about. I might have known she was a grafter, like all the rest of the crowd."

"You have no right to say that!" she reproved. "You have no right to speak so about the woman you love."

"Love?" he echoed. "Why, I don't love her. I don't love her any more than if I'd never seen her. And even if all this hadn't come up, I know now I hadn't the right to love her."

"You don't love her?" exclaimed Viva.

"No. That's God's own truth. Why should I lie about it, even to myself?"

"But you told me you loved her," persisted Viva. "You told me so. And every word and every look of yours, for months and months, has told me the same thing."

"Yes," he assented wretchedly, "I told you so. And it was true. I loved her more than everything else put together. It's good to be loved as I loved Maida. It's good to be loved so, even by a poor dub like Magnus Braith. But it's dead, now—too dead to bury. I don't love her, I tell you."

"Then you never loved her," accused Viva. "Never."

"No?" he queried ironically. "Then it was a blazing good imitation. Lord save me from the real thing, if that was a fake!"

"I tell you you never loved her," declared Viva. "If you had loved her, you would love her now, no matter what she'd done or how cruelly she had deceived you. Love can't die, any more than God can die. If you'd really loved her, you'd love her to your death-day, no matter if everyone proved to you how worthless she was. That is the difference between love and infatuation. Any petty wound can kill infatuation. But the Almighty Himself can't kill love."

"Maybe not," he assented with utter dearth of interest. "It can't matter now. And I don't feel up to talking about it yet. The reason I broke my office rule by seeing you this morning was because there was something that had to be said between us—something that isn't easy to say. That's why I wanted to get it over at once."

HER level brows quivered ever so little as she looked expectantly at him. He blundered on:

"I'm not often wrong in my snap judgments. That's why I'm where I am to-day, instead of wearing jumper and overalls. But—apart from Maida—I've made a big mistake, a mistake I've got to apologize for, because it did you a lot of injustice."

"Me?" she queried, perplexed.

"You sized her up, from the start," he answered. "I see that now. You knew what she was. You knew she was fooling me. And because you were square and clean, it riled you. And that made you snippy to her. And I, like the chucklehead I was—I thought you were sore on her because she was young and pretty and a success. And I told you so. I told you so in a rotten way. And you stood for it, without defending yourself. I judged you wrong, and you let me do it. That's what I had to say to you to-day—to tell you I understand all about it now and that I'm ashamed of myself. Not that that does any good! But you've got a right to know. Will you—will you try to forget it, Viva?"

"Please don't speak so!" she entreated, keenly pained at his abasement. "Any other man would have thought and spoken just as you did—and even more brutally. You couldn't know. I understood that, all along, and I wasn't angry or offended. Honestly, I wasn't. I was only horribly sorry for you. And I wanted to help you."

"But why didn't you, then?" he asked, struck by a new thought. "Why didn't you help me, Viva? Was it fair—was it friendly—to let me go ahead with my eyes shut?"

"I couldn't have opened them," she told him. "What had I to go on but silly feminine intuition? I had no proof. And if I'd told you what I suspected, you wouldn't have believed me. You know you wouldn't. You'd have thought even more that I was envious of younger and prettier—"

"No!" he denied vehemently, though in his heart he knew she was right.

"Besides," she continued, "I couldn't do it, on my own account. I don't quite know why. But I couldn't. I'm afraid I'm unwomanly—as you once said I was. I can't—"

"Viva!" he protested in sharp self-loathing.

"I can't do or say any of the little feminine things to set a man against another woman," she went on. "I can't make it seem honest. I'm afraid I'm more like a man, that way. I came down here to-day because it was I who unconsciously got you into all this mess. And it was only fair that I should come and say how sorry I am and to ask leave to help get you out of it, if I can. Is there anything I can do, Magnus! If there is—"

"You can forget how rotten I've been to you," he said, "and you can try to think a bit kindly of me. There won't be much competition, along Broadway, in that last part. That's all you can do. And I'll feel a whole lot better if you'll promise to do it."

"That favor was granted long before it was asked," said Viva. "And if ever you are lonely or unhappy, and if I can cheer you up at all, won't you come to see me? Please do."

"Thanks," he said. "And when I can, I'll do it. You've gotten to mean a good deal to me this past few months, Viva—more'n I realized till now. Your flat's the only home I've been in since I grew up. I didn't know business women could make a real home, till I saw yours. And once I blabbed to you about a home, thinking you wouldn't hardly know what the word meant. And all the time you had one that you'd made yourself.

"Lord, what a blind, blundering fool I've made of myself!" he railed on. "I knocked business women. And the only square, sweet girl I've ever met was a business woman. I whined for an innocent, unsophisticated girl. And the only one of those I ever met turned out to be—well, Maida Standish. I guess they don't make 'em any foolisher'n I am. Foolishness isn't on the free list. And I'm sure paying market rates for mine. I'm not speaking about the fifty thousand I've dropped, or the reputation this fake play has given me. I mean the smashing of all my dandy air-castles and—"

"There never yet was an air-castle," she said oracularly, "that hadn't its duplicate on solid earth—if only we have the patience and wit to keep on looking for it. That is true, Magnus. And you must believe it. When you were a boy, Broadway was your air-castle. You kept on till you found the reality. Then you longed for love and for a woman who would make you happy, and for a home. And—"

"And I found—Maida Standish!" was the involuntary interruption that sprang to his lips.

BUT he choked it back unspoken as Viva continued: "And you will find them all, if only you will have the patience to wait and if you will be strong enough not to let this one miserable failure kill your ideals and your hope. And I believe you *will* be strong enough, Magnus. She is waiting for you somewhere—this woman who will make up to you for what you have lost. I give you my word for that. And Magnus, all this *hasn't* been dead loss!"

"What do you mean?"

"You have lost what never existed—that is all. In return you have gained what can never be taken away from you. You are no more the rough, flashy Magnus Braith of three months ago than—than a thoroughbred racer is like a trick pony. Maida has changed you more than you realize. Your infatuation for her has brought out the real man—the fine, strong, clean man that was underneath..... And I'll—perhaps I can help you find the—the woman you have been looking for. She's waiting for you, you know, always waiting—always looking forward to the day that will bring you to her. That is the Gospel truth. I'm not just saying it to comfort you. Good-by, Magnus."

She was gone. And as he turned to the day's work, Braith was amazed and a little self-reproachful to find she had somehow contrived to awaken him from his dead apathy and to give him courage to face the day.

He wondered, vastly, at this phenomenon. An hour ago, all his life had seemed to lie behind him. He still felt stricken and dazed. But he was alive once more—alive and ready to meet the hard future, instead of brooding torturedly over the worthless past.

Yes, he would keep his word. He would go to see Viva. It was the only glint of light in the loneliness that lay ahead. She was a good friend, a good pal.

ONE day six months later Braith said to Viva quite suddenly, quite abruptly, as they sat in her little living-room:

"You've made good on that prophecy of yours, Viva. I've found the woman who could make me happy! But—but that's all the good it's liable to do me, unless—unless—"

Thus far had his abrupt start carried him. And here, all at once, his hard-spurred courage deserted him.

"Unless—" he repeated nervously.

"Unless?" she echoed, smiling up at him from under her level brows.

"Unless," he went on stammering, "unless—oh, Viva, *tell* me whether the woman who could make me happy is going to bother herself to do it! *Tell* me!"

"She has been bothering herself about you for almost a year now," Viva answered very softly. "And I'm afraid it's grown to be a life-habit—a glorious life-habit, my sweetheart."

The End

Appendix I

Notes on the Source Material

This novel was serialized in three issues of *The Green Book:*

November 1917, Chapters I through IX
December 1917, Chapters X through XVIII
January 1918, Chapters XIX through XXIV

The Green Book, November 1917

Front text
Author of "Dollars and Cents," "The Years of the Locust," etc.
[Publisher's Note: Both novels mentioned were serialized in *The Green Book*.]

End text:
THE dramatic romance of *White-light Braith* comes to its most tense situations in the next installment of Mr. Terhune's remarkable story. Be sure to get your December GREEN BOOK MAGAZINE early, for we anticipate a heavy demand for it when it goes on sale November 12th.

The Green Book, December 1917

Front text:
A Complete Résumé
Of the Opening Installment
BEDLAM and the theaters turned loose their occupants at the same moment. The garish white line of Broadway, with its harrow-teeth of side-streets from Herald Square to the Winter Garden, was the glistering receptacle into which these two elements were dumped.

Four theater-goers who stood in the thronged lobby of the Hyperion, waiting their turn for their car, were blind to the fact that they were the collective target of more interested glances than were any of the hundreds of people who hemmed them in. They were Dave Rodman, a wine-agent who was backing the show at the Hyperion; Marion Kessel, a comic-opera singer; Viva Russ, designer of stage costumes and stage settings; and Magnus Braith,—White-light Braith,—who reminded everyone of Diamond Jim Brady by spending his evenings and oodles of cash on Broadway.

At Rector's, Magnus Braith and his three guests were received with the welcome accorded only to Broadway notables. All this was fame—the fame which Braith had so avidly craved and which he now no longer noticed. As the four passed out of the dining-room, Viva Russ dropped into step at Braith's side and asked that he come to her flat for a talk.

"But it's a bunch I'm sick of," said Braith to Viva after telling how he had reached the top in the business world and how he had achieved what he had thought he wanted. "I want a home. I want to find a girl that's the kind of girl my mother used to be, out yonder in the country."

"Nothing doing," interrupted Magnus a few minutes later, after Viva had asked him to read a play written by "a budding playwright" wished on her by her father, a clergyman. As Braith, leaving, neared a pair of dark portières which separated the living-room from the bedroom adjoining, a girl stepped out.

"Good Lord!" sputtered Braith, introduced by Viva, "are you the woman who came here to sell a play?"

"I'm Maida Standish. Yes sir," replied the girl bashfully.

Braith read the 'script of "Ropes of Sand," the girl's play, before he retired that night. He pronounced it "a marvelous find." As he was about to retire, he caught a prowler in his room—Charlie Logan, the night hall-boy, who had been discharged that day. Braith let Logan go—with "a handful of chicken-feed." The next day Logan told Braith he would pay back every cent. He told Braith he had to take care of his two-year-old child because his wife had left him.

Before Braith started to work on the play, he had to convince Miss Standish that the lurid stories about him were false.

"One of them is born every minute," Maida quoted to her likeness in the mirror after Braith left, "but they must have used a whole month's supply on him."

Christmas night was the night of the première of Maida Standish's play, "Ropes of Sand," at the Halcyon Theater. Christmas had been a day of mixed feelings to Braith. He had sent an electric runabout as a gift to Maida, but she had refused to accept it. After that, he received a visit from Charlie Logan, who thanked Braith for playing Santa Claus so well to "the kid." On the way to the theater that night, Maida, glancing out of the window of the limousine, saw something which unnerved her greatly. Questioned by Viva,

Maida finally exclaimed: "It was a man. I—hate him! He was dead. Oh, he *said* he was! I mean, I—"

End text:

The conclusion of Mr. Terhune's dramatic story of New York life will appear in the January GREEN BOOK MAGAZINE—on sale December 12th.

The Green Book, January 1918

Front text:

A Complete Résumé
Of the Opening Installment

[The previous issue's Résumé was repeated this issue, followed by the next few paragraphs.]

THE premiere of Maida Standish's play was a decided success. After the performance Maida induced Braith to slip away from their party and go to Viva's flat. Just as Braith was leaving, Maida threw her arms around his neck and kissed him. Viva came into the apartment. Braith tried to explain that it all was his fault, but Viva was not convinced.

"You are playing some game I don't understand," said Viva to Maida after Braith had left.

Braith stayed up to get the morning papers, to see what the critics said of the play. And then came a severe blow to Braith—*The Chronicle's* critic charged that Maida Standish had stolen the play, almost line for line, from a play written by Dion Boucicault in 1841. Braith went to whip the critic, but came away convinced that the critic was right. Loyalty shouted within him against the judgment his common sense was seeking to render.

"I wont believe it!" he told himself desperately. "I'll go to see her, now! And—and may God help her to clear herself!"

End text:

The first story of

"The Women Tamers"

stories of the men who have been recognized by history as famous love-makers

By ALBERT PAYSON TERHUNE

will be in the next—the February—issue of
THE GREEN BOOK MAGAZINE

Note: The series in the next six issues of The Green Book was entitled "The Woman Tamers."

Captions for illustrations:

Frontis
The gallery-gods.

Page 4
Stolidly the four stood, with all the long-learned patience of true New Yorkers, waiting their turn. And all four, through this same long experience, were blind to the fact that they were the collective target of more interested glances than were any of the hundreds of people who hemmed them in.

Page 6
The twentieth New Yorker, and the stranger within the city's gates keep the lights agleam.

Page 7
No caption.

Page 8
"Those are the people in the second row I was trying to make you see this evening," he told the girl.

Page 13
They'd be hard-faced and made up and sophisticated as a barkeep. And they'd have a wife's true love for my bank-account.

Page 18
No caption.

Page 19
No caption.

Page 39
A wordless gurgle—something between a cat's snarl and a death-rattle—broke from her in the midst of her gay talk. For one flash of time, she glared into the passing foot-crowd with a face distorted and ash-gray.

Page 41
No caption.

Page 43
"It isn't the managers—is it?—who accept or reject a play: it's the first-nighters." "Not always," Braith corrected her. "And even then, it's just a dozen or so of the first-nighters that count—the vivisection squad."

Page 44
The audience, by this time, was unmistakably and whole-heartedly with the author and her brainchild.

Page 45
The orchestra—another Old World relic at the Halcyon—was tuning for the overture.

Page 53
Half aloud, he read: "It would be pleasant enough to fall into a woman's arms, if one did not fall into her hands at the same time."

Page 54
A little clock somewhere in the bedroom behind her broke into a soft cadence of chimes. "It's twelve o'clock," breathed Maida. "Twelve o'clock! It's your birthday, Magnus!"

Page 76
The last of the White Way cabbies.

Page 81
"What's the idea?" Braith heard a lounger ask. "The show didn't open until last night." "Boss' orders," was the laconic response. "It's canned."

Page 83
The ex-convict accosted him with a broad and congratulatory grin. "Good work, brother!" he approved cordially. "It was framed as slick as anyone would want."

Page 88
Between set teeth he forced the question: "Will you marry me?"

Page 90
"Juries have a cunning little way of taking a pretty woman's word, and of letting her face decide their verdict instead of waiting for evidence."

Page 92
In nightmares nothing surprises us. We are frightened or benumbed, according to our nature, when the three-headed elephant charges down upon us.

Page 101
"There won't be any more noise," she heard herself murmur: and into her mind came fantastically the death-speech of *Hamlet: "The rest is silence!"* She sat down, holding her baby's likeness again before her tortured eyes.

General notes

The modern reader will find certain conventions in this 1917 novel odd, perhaps even startling. One example is a combination of both comma and em-dash for an abrupt pause. For the most part, the original styles have been retained. However, the following alterations *were* made for this edition:

The word **won't** (when used for "will not") was consistently spelled without an apostrophe. We have inserted that helpful mark.

Similarly, the apostrophe was missing from **ain't,** and was inserted for that word also, to make it conform to proper English.

The following line in Chapter XIV:
Strangled with weeping, she ran blindly down the hall to her own room, slamming and locking the door behind me.

...was changed to:

Strangled with weeping, she ran blindly down the hall to her own room, slamming and locking the door behind her.

Clyde Fitch (1865 – 1909), mentioned in this novel, was a highly popular writer of Broadway plays during the last decade of the 19th Century, and the first decade of the 20th. He died of complications related to appendicitis at the height of his career.

The subtitle of this book is "A Novel of New York's Broadway." In the original, it was simply, "A Novel of New York."

The photograph on the cover is from the Library of Congress, www.loc.gov/item/det1994021937/PP/, which it identifies as "Times Square at night, New York, N.Y.," and estimates the date "between 1900 and 1915." It further states, "No known restrictions on publication."

stuffnobodycaresabout.com/2016/03/28/old-new-york-photos-61/ does a good job at analyzing when the cover photo (and another) were taken. Their estimate is 1912. This photo was the closest to the time of this novel that the publisher could find.

Appendix II

An Atrocity No Publisher Should Attempt

Suppose...

Suppose there were part of this story that Mr. Terhune had left untold. For whatever reason.

Suppose... it directly followed Chapter XIII, and that it went something like...

...*this:*

CHAPTER XIII.I

"Mr. Braith!"

Magnus paused at the foot of the outside steps and turned to Logan. They had descended the ten flights in grim silence. The elevator-boy, seeing the two men's expressions as they entered the cart, had instinctively known to keep his own silence, and with every furtive glance he'd stolen, had grown more terrified as they plummeted to ground level.

"I must thank you again, Mr. Braith—"

"None of that!" Braith said dismissively, raising a hand.

"But Mr. Braith," Logan persisted miserably, "I *wanted* to kill her. I *really* wanted to kill her. The mother of my son!"

"That's why I stopped you," Magnus said gently. "I *knew* you would have."

"Then I—"

In quick succession came three sounds.

THUMP!

"Owwwww!" Logan ducked and put both hands to his hat.

CLINK-clatter-clatter-clatter...

"Logan! What in the name of— Are you all right?"

"Something hit my head," Logan said. "If I weren't wearing my hat— Ouch!" He scanned the sidewalk. "What?— Where?—"

"Here!" Magnus bent over, straightened, holding an object. It was a small bottle of thick, tinted glass.

"Some damn fool throwing his trash out the window!" Logan had his hat off, and was rubbing his head. He looked up.

"Logan!"

Logan glanced sharply at Braith, frowning at the abrupt tone in the man's voice.

"This has Maida's name on it."

Logan's frown deepened.

"It's a prescription," Braith went on. "For morphia sulphate."

"But what's—"

"And it's empty."

Logan and Braith held each other's eyes tensely.

"I still say she deserves to die," Logan said with conviction.

Braith inhaled slowly but did not answer.

"She's not worth saving."

Braith said nothing.

Logan looked down at the concrete. "I—I'd be a fool to do anything—to try—" He shook his head slowly, perplexedly.

He looked up at Braith.

Braith's expression was difficult to read. Few would consider his mouth to be smiling; yet it was free of anger, fury, or any form of dissatisfaction. The eyes bored into Logan's with the hardness and coldness of a granite drill, yet held no accusation or condemnation. Whatever that expression could be called, or whether it were possible to even name it with one word, Logan realized that Braith fully knew what was about to happen next.

Logan ran up the stairs, taking three steps at a stride, and disappeared back into the building. Magnus climbed the steps and saw Logan punching furiously at the elevator call-button. Logan threw his head back, as if forcing his vision to pierce ten floors. Then, he leapt onto the adjoining stairway and was gone, the staccato of his footsteps echoing in the stairwell.

Magnus Braith took the outside steps in two leaps. Standing on the concrete, arms slightly akimbo and seeming taller than usual with his neck craned, he scanned the crowded street, left, right. Then he raised a hand.

"Officer!" he shouted, his powerful voice cutting through the city clamor. Faces turned toward him, including that of the policeman. *"Officer! The nearest call box, please! I need you to make a call!"*

As Braith made through the crowd, there was no mistaking the urgency in his body's motion. A few whom he rushed past were able to glimpse his face and would later recall and wonder at the smile of exultant satisfaction they saw there.

Other books available
from the Silver Creek Press

2016
The Woman Tamers,
by Albert Payson Terhune
Six essays on heart-breakers of the past.

In Treason's Track,
by Albert Payson Terhune
A novel of the American Revolution.

2015
The Flood Fighters,
by Albert Payson Terhune
A novel first serialized in Country Gentleman magazine in 1920,
published under a pseudonym and not reprinted until now.

An Albert Payson Terhune Reader
27 stories by Terhune from pulp magazines of the 1910s and 20s,
featuring all original illustrations.

(The above are available from the major bookstores online, both as print
books and as e-books.)

2006
*The Park Avenue Hunt Club:
The Silver Creek Edition*
by Judson Phillips and Rodney Schroeter
(Available from the publisher)

Forthcoming
More work by Albert Payson Terhune
that has not seen print since its original publication.
More pulp fiction from the early 20th Century
by various authors.